'I'm sorry,' Connie sighed.

'It's just—getting to me.'

'I can imagine. Don't apologise. Just take the pills, drink the drink and go back to bed with a book. You'll be asleep in no time.'

She snorted. 'I wouldn't bet on it. I haven't been able to sleep for weeks, so I don't imagine you'll be able to work a miracle with your hot milk and happy pills.'

Patrick chuckled. 'It's worth a try. What do you want me to do, read you a bedtime story?'

Make love to me, she nearly said, and then felt herself colour.

D1426267

Caroline Anderson's nursing career was brought to an abrupt halt by a back injury, but her interest in medical things led her to work first as a medical secretary and then, after completing her teacher training, as a lecturer in Medical Office Practice to trainee medical secretaries. She lives in rural Suffolk with her husband, two daughters, and assorted animals.

Recent titles by the same author:

AN UNEXPECTED BONUS
SARAH'S GIFT
CAPTIVE HEART
DEFINITELY MAYBE
THAT FOREVER FEELING

PRACTICALLY PERFECT

BY
CAROLINE ANDERSON

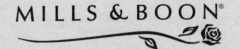

All the characters in this book have no existence outside the imagination of the author, and have no relation whatsoever to anyone bearing the same name or names. They are not even distantly inspired by any individual known or unknown to the author, and all the incidents are pure invention.

First published in Great Britain 1999
Harlequin Mills & Boon Limited,
Eton House, 18-24 Paradise Road, Richmond, Surrey TW9 1SR

© Caroline Anderson 1999

ISBN 0 263 81814 4

Set in Times Roman 10½ on 12 pt.
03-9910-48580-D

Printed and bound in Spain
by Litografia Rosés S.A., Barcelona

CHAPTER ONE

THE village was as dark as pitch, the few streetlights long since extinguished. Connie struggled for her purse in the bottomless pit of her handbag and tugged out a few notes for the taxi driver.

'Got any change, love?' he asked. 'I'm a bit short tonight.'

She debated searching her bag again for loose coins and dismissed the idea. The clatter of the diesel engine was rattling the windows in all the houses, and any minute now lights would start to come on.

'Forget it,' she told him, dredging up a weary smile. 'Don't worry about the change. Thank you.'

'Sure? Cheers, then,' he said with a grin, and she watched his tail lights disappear, taking the clatter with it. The silence of the night settled back around her like a familiar blanket, and she scooped up her luggage, struggled to find her keys with her uncooperative and useless hand and let herself in.

A wave of fur and slurping tongues assaulted her, and she chuckled and sat down on the bottom step, letting them get it out of their systems. The dogs sniffed her plaster cast curiously, licking her numb, stiff fingers with care, as if they sensed all was not quite well. 'Good boys,' she whispered. 'Now go and lie down.'

Their tails lashed, and she bumped and trailed upstairs with her luggage, the dogs hopefully in tow.

'Oh, all right, then, just this once,' she scolded

gently, and let them into her bedroom. They were settled on the end of her bed before she'd put on the
light, and it took her almost as long to shuck her outer
clothes, flick off the light and slide under the covers.

She'd wash in the morning. She didn't want to disturb her parents—not in the middle of the night, and
not with all the explanations she'd have to give them.
She snuggled down, shifting Rolo so her legs could
stretch out, and Toby curled up against her side, his
head under her hand, and gave a heavy sigh. She fin-
gered the soft tufts of fur on his head, taking comfort
from his warmth and presence, and after a few moments she fell asleep.

'What is it, boys? Can you hear something?'

She pushed herself upright and listened, and sure
enough there was a clonk and a thud downstairs, followed by a muffled curse.

How odd. What was her father doing up at this
time—unless he was on call, of course, but she thought
he'd arranged night cover and only did the odd bit at
weekends now out of hours?

Still befuddled by sleep, she slipped her legs over
the edge of the bed and tiptoed to the door, listening.
The dogs whined softly, tails waving, making a
draught on her bare legs. 'Stay,' she told them, and
opened the door, stepping silently out onto the landing.

Light spilled from the dining room, casting an eerie
glow up the walls. There was another thud followed
by a string of colourful prose, and she crept to the
edge of the stairs and peered over, just in time to see
a figure in jeans and a leather jacket disappear through
the connecting door to the surgery premises, flicking
on the lights as bold as brass.

A quick frown pleated her brow, and without a thought she sneaked down the stairs, the dogs at her feet, and edged up to the surgery door. More banging, another string of impolite adjectives in a deep, frustrated voice, then silence. She looked around for something to use as a club, and her eyes fell on her brother's cricket bat in the umbrella stand by the front door.

Excellent. She tiptoed across the hall and eased it carefully from the stand, testing the grip with her left hand. Good.

Then she glanced into the brightly lit dining room and her jaw dropped.

The dresser shelves were empty!

The silver was gone, the Georgian tea service, the platters, the ladle, the candlesticks—and the carriage clock from the mantelpiece.

Anger tightened her grip on the club, and without hesitation she went swiftly to the surgery door, slipped through it and edged round the corner. He was in Reception, his back to her, reaching up into the cupboard where her father kept the controlled drugs, and with more courage than sense she crept up behind him. Grief, he was huge! So tall, and the leather jacket was strained taut over those broad shoulders as he rummaged in the cupboard.

Eyeing a spot in the centre of his thick, dark hair, she raised the cricket bat over her head and brought it down on his skull with a resounding *thunk*.

He gave a startled yelp and ducked, his hands flying up to protect himself against further blows, and then before she could move again she found herself grabbed and her left arm twisted firmly up behind her back. Her front slammed into the wall of neatly filed patient notes, her nose wedged somewhere in the Ds, and a powerful hand relieved her of the cricket bat and then turned her round, pushing her down onto the floor.

'Sit,' he growled, and she sat, awkwardly, peering up into furious grey eyes and wondering if she could reach the panic button under the edge of the desk. The dogs, useless as ever, had failed to come with her, knowing they weren't allowed into the surgery area. Why couldn't they have used their initiative for once? He was a burglar, for heaven's sake—

'Where is it?' she asked, leaping in yet again where angels would have had more sense. 'What have you done with it?'

His brow creased. 'Done with what?'

'The silver.'

The scowl deepened. 'I don't know what the hell you're talking about, young lady, but I think we'll save your explanations for the police.' He reached for the phone, one hand gingerly feeling his skull.

'Police?' She stared at him. 'Why would you call the police?'

He shot her a jaundiced, disbelieving look. 'Because a pint-sized, half-naked adolescent has just accosted me with a club and tried to steal the drugs?'

She glanced down, and hot colour flooded her cheeks. She rearranged her legs, but nothing could make the T-shirt longer or hide the kitten-print knickers which were all she'd had left until she did some washing. No wonder he thought she was a teenager! But drugs—?

'*You* broke in—*you* were stealing the drugs,' she reminded him crossly. '*And* the silver.'

He rolled his eyes. 'That again. I don't know anything about any silver, and I have no need to break in. I've got the keys.'

Her eyes widened in shock. 'Why? What have you done to my father?'

He stared at her for a moment, his eyes narrowed, searching, and then with a groan he ran his hand over his face and looked at her again.

'Connie?' he said softly.

She straightened. 'How did you know my name?' she asked, stunned and a little confused.

'So you are the missing daughter?'

'Missing? I'm not missing, I'm here.' What did he mean—missing? Panic assailed her. 'Where is he?' she cried, half getting to her feet. 'What have you done to my father?'

He lowered the telephone and sighed. 'I haven't done anything to him—I'm the locum. Patrick Durrant. And you're Connie.'

'Locum?' Connie's bravado wilted in a pile of gloop. They must be on holiday—again. 'Oh, lawks,' she muttered.

'Lawks, indeed. So, are you Connie?'

She nodded miserably. 'Yes—and I suppose I owe you an apology.'

He snorted. 'Don't strain yourself.'

'Well, the silver *is* missing, and you *were* rummaging in the controlled drugs, not to mention creeping around in the dark.'

'Hardly rummaging. I'm replacing the stock of diamorphine in my bag before I forget, and the bulb's gone in the hall light.' He eyed her thoughtfully. 'I don't suppose you'd like to take a look at my head, would you? Assuming, of course, that you've got over your urge to kill me.' He felt again, and his fingertips came away covered in blood.

Connie closed her eyes. She was going to prison, she just knew it. How could she have *done* anything so crazy? Dear God, she might easily have killed him!

'You don't look like a doctor,' she said in her defence.

He arched a brow, clearly stifling a laugh. 'And you do?'

She scrambled to her feet awkwardly, trying not to use her injured arm, and his eyes tracked to it and to her T-shirt, hovering somewhere between her bare midriff and the skinny jut of her hipbones. The silly knickers taunted her from underneath, and she tugged the hem of her T-shirt fruitlessly.

A smile quirked at the corner of his mouth. 'Why don't you go and slip into something a little more substantial while I boil the kettle? I think we might both have a little explaining to do.'

'What about your head?'

'It'll keep,' he said, and shooed her out. 'Go on, hop it. Get dressed.'

She didn't need to be told twice!

Patrick studied the empty doorway in bemused silence for a moment. Her scent lingered on the air, the only thing that remained of their encounter—that and the egg on his head. For someone so tiny and delicate-looking, she sure packed a hell of a wallop. His fingers sought out the rapidly rising lump on his head, and he winced and swore again.

Good job it had been her left arm she'd used. If her right hadn't been safely tucked up out of the way in a plaster cast, she might have done him some real damage, for all she was so tiny.

He prodded and winced again, then, easing himself off the edge of the desk, he finished what he'd been doing with the drugs, locked up again, then went through into the kitchen, filled the kettle and switched it on. He took his jacket off, dropped it over the back of a chair, and then he sat down, suddenly woozy.

'Not concussion,' he muttered, resting his head on his arms. 'Please, God, not concussion. I hate throwing up.'

A waft of that scent drifted into his consciousness—not something soft and delicate and flowery and appropriate, but a deep, musky, sensual blend of something exotic and powerful, something totally unsuitable and all woman that sent his pulse rate into warp drive and did terrifying things to his already fragile head.

He tried to sit up.

'Stay there,' she ordered, and he felt the delicate touch of her fingers through his hair, sifting, probing, gently checking out the damage. There was something strangely erotic about her touch, about the feel of her fingers in his hair, and he fantasised about being held against her soft, slender body while her hands glided sensuously—

'Ouch! Dammit, be careful!'

'Sorry. I think you'll live. Let me see your eyes.'

He lifted his head and stared into twin pools of deep honey brown the colour of autumn. Silky strands of red-gold hair tumbled round her shoulders, skittering into her eyes and irritating her. She scooped it out of the way with an impatient hand, anchoring it behind her ears, and studied his pupils with intensity.

He studied her with just as much intensity, wondering how his body could react so cheerfully and whole heartedly to her when she'd just minutes before tried to deck him with a cricket bat.

'What?' Connie demanded, straightening up. 'Why are you laughing?'

'Was I?'

She subsided into a chair opposite. 'I think so. You need ice on that.'

'I don't doubt it. There's a cold pack in the fridge in the dispensary.'

'I'll get it.'

She went, and he watched her, absorbed by the sexy sway of her slim but definitely feminine hips, the way the jeans hugged her bottom like a lover...

He groaned and dropped his head onto his arms again. He was jealous of her jeans, for heaven's sake! How could he be jealous of her jeans? Maybe he should put the cold pack down his trousers.

'You're losing it, Durrant,' he growled.

'Losing what?'

His head jerked up, nearly splitting open, and he groaned again and closed his eyes. 'Don't sneak up on me. I hurt too much.'

'I'm sorry.'

Patrick opened his eyes again and saw the guilt and remorse written on her fine-boned face. Her eyes were huge pools of regret, and her teeth caught her lip and gnawed it anxiously.

'I'm going to live, you know.'

'I know. I just feel...'

'I can imagine. Does it need stitches?'

She went suddenly still, a curious deadness overlaying the regret. Her voice was stiff and remote. 'No—or glueing. It's fine. It's just a little split.'

'In the bone?' he asked drily, and her mouth twisted into what might have been a smile.

'No, probably not,' she said. 'Lucky for you I've broken this, or I would have hit you harder.' She gestured with her hand. Her right hand. The one with the cast on it. The one she couldn't stitch with?

He jerked his head at it. 'What happened?'

She looked down at her arm, and her face closed again. 'I fell,' she said economically.

He wondered what she wasn't telling, and where she'd been for the past two weeks, and why her parents hadn't known she'd broken it. From the look on her face, there was a lot she wasn't telling.

Yet.

He stood up carefully, taking the cold pack and wrapping it in a clean teatowel before offering it cautiously to his skull. Hmm. Hurt like the dickens, but at least his vision was clearing. All he needed was something to eat and drink—

'Cup of tea?' he suggested.

She jumped up and rushed over to the kettle. 'I'll do it—you sit down.'

He did, quite happy to retreat to the chair before he fell over. His head was pounding like a steam hammer, and he felt sick again. He held the cold pack over the lump and leaned his arm on the table, watching her as she bustled about with the tea.

So this was the girl Tom Wright was so proud of— his valedictorian progeny with a brilliant career ahead of her in paediatric surgery. And she thought *he* didn't look like a doctor!

She couldn't have been any bigger than some of her patients. He wondered if she had difficulty making people take her seriously. Perhaps she always carried the cricket bat as a persuader, to keep people in order.

A smile touched his mouth and he suppressed a chuckle, just as she spun on her heel and dumped the mugs on the table. 'Biscuit?' she offered, and he nodded. Maybe it would settle his stomach, but he doubted it. He somehow thought he wasn't going to get away with it.

'I can only find custard creams,' she announced from the depths of the cupboard. 'Will they do?'

She pulled herself out, brandishing the packet, and he felt the colour drain from his face.

'I think I'll pass,' he muttered, and then everything went black.

'Oh, hell.' Connie scrambled to her feet and went over to him. Patrick was slumped against the table, out cold, and she wanted to get him flat and raise his feet. She eyed the floor, quarry-tiled and unyielding, and wondered if she'd do him more damage by dropping him on it than by leaving him alone.

He must weigh nearly twice what she did, and she didn't fancy her chances of lowering him carefully into the recovery position.

He took the decision out of her hands by sliding, very slowly and tidily, off the chair and onto the floor at her feet. She caught his head just before it cracked against the tiles, and eased him out straight, the dogs sniffing round and taking too much interest.

'Shoo,' she told them, then she wadded up his leather jacket under his head and smoothed the hair off his brow. Should she call an ambulance?

She felt his pulse, strong and regular and about the right speed, and checked his pupils, equal and both reactive to the light, then sat back on her heels. She'd give him another minute. If he still hadn't come round, she'd call for help. In the meantime—

His eyes flickered open, a clear, steady grey, and he groaned and shut them again. 'I hate concussion,' he muttered.

Well, at least he knew what was going on. 'What's your name?' she asked him.

'Patrick Durrant. I told you that. Stop testing me, I'm all right. I just feel sick.'

'Pins and needles?'

'No—and I haven't got double vision and I haven't got a severe headache. Connie, I'm fine. I just haven't eaten for twenty-four hours, I've been too busy.'

She sat back again on her heels and huffed a sigh. 'Well, for goodness' sake, no wonder you fainted! You had me worried half to death!'

He cracked an eye open and studied her for a moment. 'What's the matter—don't you fancy being had up on a murder charge?'

She resisted the urge to hit him again, just because he'd got too close to the mark. Instead she helped him back into the chair, gave him a minute to recover and then steadied him as he walked cautiously through to the sitting room and stretched out full length on the sofa.

'I'll cook you something simple. Stay here.'

'As if I'm going anywhere,' he muttered, and his eyes slid shut again.

She threw together some scrambled eggs and toast, prodded him awake and fed him, and then covered him when he dozed off, feet dangling over the end, one arm hanging by his side, the back of his hand trailing on the carpet.

He looked tired and vulnerable and defenceless, and Connie felt another wave of guilt wash over her. Still, what was she supposed to do—ask a burglar for his credentials before hitting him?

Or, perhaps, just call the police like a normal person would instead of wading in there in her underwear and clubbing him over the head!

Oh, damn.

She couldn't leave him, so she went upstairs and took the quilt off her bed and dragged it downstairs, snuggling in it on a big, comfy chair in the soft light of a table lamp. The dogs settled down at her feet, curled together on the edge of the quilt, and she lay and listened to the homely sound of Patrick's breathing, the odd soft snore punctuating the steady and even sigh of his breath.

Every now and then she got up and checked him, making sure that the concussion hadn't deepened and that he was still only asleep and not unconscious. At five, when he was sleeping particularly heavily, she shone a torch in his eyes to check his pupils and elicited a stream of invective.

'You'll do,' she said, and curled up again, dozing fitfully. At six, after a total of about two hours' sleep, she rose stiffly from the chair, let the dogs out in the garden and put the kettle on.

She was in the bedroom overhead when she heard him stirring, and she went down again and found him sitting up on the edge of the sofa, his legs braced apart and his elbows propped, a wry smile on his face.

'Are you all right?' Connie asked cautiously, not altogether sure she wanted the answer.

'I'll live.'

'Headache?'

'Just a tad. Are you making tea?'

She nodded.

'Not too strong, dash of milk, no sugar,' he told her, and unravelling himself from the remains of the quilt he headed for the door. She moved out of his way, but a warm, musky, male scent lingered on the air, teasing her senses.

She chewed her lip. She must be crazy thinking about him like that—apart from anything else he wouldn't be interested in someone who'd tried to kill him! She went into the kitchen and made the tea, but while it was brewing there was a crash from upstairs.

'Oh, my God,' she muttered, and headed for the stairs at a flat-out run. If he'd fallen in the bathroom and hit his head again... She grabbed the knob and twisted it, throwing the door open, and met Patrick's bemused and patient expression.

'Oh,' she said weakly. 'You're all right. I heard a crash.'

'I knocked the shampoo bottle into the bath.'

'Oh. Thank God for that. I thought you'd passed out.'

She sagged against the doorframe, then belatedly realised that he had just stepped out of the shower. Without her permission her eyes ran down his very wet and naked body, and with a little gasp she dragged her eyes back up to his face and jack knifed away from the wall. 'Sorry—I'll—er—leave you to it. Tea's ready.'

His mouth quirked in a smile that could just have been patronising, and she spun on her heel and shot back downstairs, nearly falling over the dogs. Why hadn't she merely knocked and asked if he was all right? Why barge in there without warning?

What was it about him that had her taking leave of her senses?

Connie poured the tea, trying hard not to think about the sleek, muscular body, the gleaming beads of water dribbling into rivers on his skin, tracking down through the damp curls that scattered his chest and arrowed down—

Oh, hell. She sat down with her mug, cradling it in both hands and blowing bubbles round on the surface. She needed to get out more. If she had a real life— one with a man in it—then the sight of him would have done nothing to her.

No. Not even she could get away with such a bare-faced lie. But even so, if she had a real life, she wouldn't have been quite so...

Awestruck?

She groaned and sipped her tea. No wonder he'd thought she was an adolescent.

She heard his heavy, even tread in the hall, and the door swung open. Patrick came in, clad in trousers and a white shirt, looking very respectable except for the wet hair dribbling water down the back of his neck and wetting his collar.

She pushed his mug towards him. 'Here, drink this before it's cold.'

He hooked the chair out with his foot and straddled it, dangling the mug in his fingertips. 'So where have you been?' he asked without preamble.

'This morning?' she asked, surprised.

'No. The past week or so.'

'Oh.' She looked down into her tea. 'Yorkshire. Why?'

'They were trying to contact you.'

'To tell me they were going on holiday again, I

suppose, in case I decided to turn up. Is it going to be a problem, me being here?'

He shook his head. 'No, not at all. But—ah—they aren't exactly on holiday.'

Something about the way he said it sent chills down her spine. 'What do you mean?' she asked, searching his face for any clues. It was craggy and interesting and—compassionate?

'Your father's had an operation—a coronary artery bypass. He's fine now, out of Intensive Care, but I think they'd like to talk to you.'

She felt the blood drain from her face. 'A bypass?'

'Four, actually. He had a quadruple. He's in Cambridge—I've got the number. You can ring them.'

She stared at him, utterly stunned. 'But—a quadruple bypass? That was sudden.'

'Not really. He's had a couple of heart attacks in the past year—just minor ones, but enough to be worrying. He's had angina for years.'

Connie felt dreadful. She'd been so busy, so absorbed with her own career, that she hadn't even noticed her father going downhill. 'I thought they just went on holiday a lot—why didn't they tell me?'

Patrick's shoulders lifted expressively. 'Maybe they didn't want to worry you. It's quite possible.'

'They should have told me.' She stood up, pacing restlessly to the sink and staring out at the garden. The signs were there, if she just bothered to look. Her father's vegetable garden, always so neatly tended and productive, was lying fallow except for a row of spinach that had gone to seed. No leeks, no onions, no cabbages of different sorts—none of the late summer or early autumn veg that he was so proud of and so successful with.

Connie closed her eyes and swallowed a little spurt of panic. 'He is all right, isn't he?' she asked in a small voice.

She didn't hear Patrick move, just felt the warm comfort of his hands cupping her shoulders. 'He's fine—truly. I saw him at the weekend. He's doing well.' He drew her back against him, and with a shaky sigh she leaned into him and took advantage of the silent support.

'I needed to get away—I had some thinking to do. I dropped off the map for a few days.'

'This?' he asked softly. His hand ran down her right arm and came to rest under her cast, his hand cupping it, his fingers warm over the numb, stiff skin of her fingers.

'Amongst other things,' she said, and moved away, not ready yet to talk to him about it. 'I ought to ring my mother—have you got the number?'

'Sure.'

He went out of the kitchen, and she sagged against the worktop and pressed her fingers to her eyes. A quadruple bypass, for heaven's sake, and they hadn't been able to get hold of her to tell her! Guilt swamped her, and she bit back a moan of reproach.

'Don't beat yourself up over it,' he advised, coming back in. 'I told them ages ago they ought to tell you what was going on, but they didn't want to worry you.'

'But I should have been there for them.'

'Like they were there for you?'

Her eyes flew up and met his, then skittered away. 'That's different,' she said hastily. 'Right, I'll ring them. How's your head now, by the way?'

He grinned, a little lopsidedly. 'It's fine. I shouldn't bother to tell them, if I were you.'

Connie laughed without humour. 'Don't worry, I wasn't about to.' She gestured at the piece of paper he'd given her, her mother's delicate spidery writing scrawled across it. 'Will she be at this number now?'

He checked his watch. 'Possibly. It's the guest house where she's staying.'

She debated going into the sitting room, but decided not to bother. Instead she hitched herself up on the worktop, took the phone off the wall and dialled the number. Moments later her mother was put on the line, and she seemed relieved to talk to Connie.

'How are you?' she asked. 'We couldn't track you down.'

'Sorry, I was in Yorkshire. How's Dad?'

'Fine—progressing really well. So how did you get the number? Did you ring us?'

'No—I came home to see you.'

'Ah. You've met Patrick, then? Are you getting on all right?'

Did she imagine it, or was there a hint of curiosity in her mother's voice? Curiosity and—hope?

She shot a glance across at Patrick and stifled a laugh. 'Yes, we're getting on fine,' she said. Apart from the cold pack on his head and her guilty conscience.

'By the way,' she added as an afterthought, 'where's the silver?'

'Oh, I packed it all up and took it in to be cleaned and valued for insurance. Why—darling, surely you didn't think Patrick had taken it?' Her mother's bright, tinkling laugh made Connie ashamed. 'Connie, he's like family. I'd trust him with anything—heavens, I'd trust him with you!'

'Oh. Good.' She met Patrick's eyes, one brow arched cynically, and felt herself colour. 'I just wondered. Look, give Dad my love. I'll try and come up to see you later today—I'll get the directions from Patrick.'

'Good,' her mother said warmly. 'Your father will be pleased to see you—I don't think he'll believe you're all right until he's seen you with his own eyes.'

Connie chatted for a few more moments, then replaced the phone.

'All right?' Patrick asked.

'Fine.' She looked down at her hand, lying useless in her lap. 'What do I tell them?' she asked him.

'About the silver? About my head? About your horribly suspicious mind?'

She shook her head, ignoring the bitterness in his voice. 'About my arm—about my hand. I didn't want to worry them, but my mother says my father won't believe I'm all right until he sees me with his own eyes.'

'And?'

'I don't know. I just know I can't go and visit my father without him noticing the cast.'

Patrick eyed her thoughtfully. 'Is there a reason you don't want them to know?'

She gave a soft, humourless laugh. 'I was being stupid. I took a risk. They hate it when I do that—so I just don't tell them. And now they're going to know.'

And, without waiting for his response, she slid off the worktop and headed for the door.

CHAPTER TWO

PATRICK let Connie go. There didn't seem to be any point in following her, and, besides, he was still feeling irritated about the silver.

His head wasn't feeling all that brilliant either. He propped his chin on his hands and sighed. He ought to eat something—that had been half his trouble yesterday—but he just didn't feel like cooking. He'd bought some nice crunchy cereal with dried raspberries in it. Perhaps he'd have some of that.

And perhaps he ought to go after Connie and talk to her. He made some fresh tea and took it through to the sitting room where he could hear her moving around. She was clearing up the cushions and quilts from their impromptu camping session, and she looked up at him with her wary honey-gold eyes.

'I've brought you some tea,' he told her. He put the mugs down on the coffee-table and took the quilt out of her arms, putting it down on the chair. Then he sat on the sofa and patted the cushion beside him. 'Come and tell Uncle Patrick all about it.'

She sat, stiffly and staring straight ahead, her colour up a little. 'Look, first of all, about the silver,' she began, but he found he didn't care about that, just about Connie and what had happened.

'Forget the silver,' he cut in. 'Tell me about your arm.'

'My arm.' Her voice was strained, and he sensed she was holding herself on a tight leash.

'Why don't you start at the beginning?' he suggested.

So she did, but it wasn't what he'd been expecting at all. 'My brother Anthony was a doctor,' she began. 'He was training to be a surgeon, and rumour had it he was tipped for the top. He just had a gift—you know the way some people do?'

Patrick nodded. 'Yes, I know, I trained with someone like that. So what happened?'

'He died. A skiing accident. He was a bit of an idiot sometimes, but a very good skier. He went off-piste with a friend, and they didn't come back. They didn't find their bodies till the spring thaw. They'd been caught in an avalanche.'

Patrick closed his eyes. To lose your brother was bad enough. To not know, for weeks, months even, what had happened must have been horrendous. 'I'm sorry,' he said gruffly. 'That must have been very difficult for all of you.'

'It was. That's why my parents are a bit overprotective. I was just starting my clinical training, and I'd intended to do paediatric medicine. Then, somehow, I just felt I had to do surgery for Anthony, so I changed the direction of my training and here I am—on the threshold of my career as a neonatal paediatric surgeon, and I go and do something stupid like this.'

'How bad is it?'

'Well, not wonderful. I damaged the nerves—I just have to wait for them to heal and recover. I'm not a patient person.'

He eyed her thoughtfully. 'How long ago did you break it?'

'Six weeks.'

'And there's still residual nerve damage?'

'It's just bruising,' she said firmly. 'It'll recover. It just takes time.'

She was an intelligent, educated woman. She was a doctor. She knew the score. So why was she deluding herself?

'And if it doesn't?'

She stiffened. 'It will. It has to.'

'But if it doesn't?' he persisted. 'Will you be able to operate?'

'Of course. It's early days to be so defeatist. I'm sure it will be fine—it's just taking time.'

OK, so she had blinkers on. It wasn't his job to tell her she was wrong. He got back to the core business. 'How did you break it?'

She looked down at it, hefting the cast as if testing its weight. 'I fell, rock-climbing. I reached out for a hold on the way past, jammed my hand into a crack and kept on going. It broke.'

Patrick winced, seeing it all too clearly for comfort. 'I imagine it would. Were you on your own?'

Connie snorted. 'Only idiots go rock-climbing on their own.'

He thought only idiots went rock-climbing, full stop, but there you go. One born every minute. 'So, what happened next?'

'They hoisted me up so they could free my arm, splinted it and helped me back down to a ledge. Then they got me airlifted off and into hospital. I had it pinned and plated, but the nerves were torn and crushed. It'll be several months before they recover as well as they're going to.'

'But they think they'll recover enough for you to go back to surgery.' He watched her, noting the tiny flinch as he said the words. There had been a wealth of pain and disappointment in her voice, carefully hidden by her matter-of-fact delivery. He sensed she needed to scream and rant and rail against fate. Perhaps that was what she'd been doing in Yorkshire. If so, he thought, she'd come back too soon.

She shrugged slightly, and reached for her tea. 'Hopefully, but not yet, of course. Neonatal paediatric surgery is very fast, very precise, very finely tuned, by definition. There's no room for clumsiness or slowness. The babies would just die—they're too frail to wait while you fiddle about. I couldn't take that responsibility.'

'How long ago did it happen? Six weeks, did you say?'

'Give or take the odd day.'

Long enough for her to know in her heart of hearts that things weren't looking good. No wonder she'd run away to Yorkshire. He reached out and touched her shoulder. 'Connie, I'm sorry.'

She stiffened, bracing herself against the sympathy that she wasn't strong enough to deal with. 'I'm fine, I just have to occupy myself until I'm better,' she said brightly, but he wasn't fooled.

He sat back with his tea and watched her over the rim, saying nothing, letting her get herself back under control. She was hanging on by a thread, and he had an insane urge to wrap his arms round her and lie to her and tell her it would be all right.

Crazy. She didn't need him to comfort her, and he certainly didn't need to get involved with her and all her problems. He had more than enough of his own.

He frowned. Why was he even thinking about getting involved with her? He must be mad. It was that bump on the head that had done it.

He stood up. 'I must get on—I'm taking surgery in half an hour. I'm going to have some breakfast—want to join me?'

'I'm not hungry. I'll have something later.'

He held his tongue. It wasn't up to him to tell her she was too thin. She'd probably take it the wrong way and bite his head off,. anyway.

Butt out, Durrant, he told himself. Go and eat and get yourself into the surgery and do the job you're here for. Connie Wright isn't your problem.

Connie watched his back disappear through the door and blinked back the threatening tears. She'd had the most insane urge to throw herself into his arms and howl her eyes out, but it was the last thing he wanted or needed—and, anyway, she'd just thumped him over the head and accused him of running off with the family silver, so she could hardly expect a favourable response!

Her stomach rumbled, and moments later she smelt the enticing and irresistible smell of frying bacon. She laughed. She knew countless vegetarians who said bacon was their only weak spot, and she could see why.

Giving in to the inevitable, she went through to the kitchen and propped up the doorway. 'Got any spare?'

He threw her a grin over his shoulder. 'How did I know you'd say that?' he teased, putting two plates down on the table next to a pile of buttered toast.

She eyed the scrambled egg sprinkled with chopped bacon and grilled tomato wedges with enthusiasm. 'Don't suppose you've put any coffee on?'

'Of course. Tuck in—it'll be ready in a moment.'

She didn't need two invitations. She dived into the plateful, using her left hand only for the—conveniently—forkable food, sipped the fragrant coffee when he handed it to her and then started on the already buttered toast.

'I thought you weren't hungry?' Patrick said calmly as she demolished another piece of toast.

'I'm a woman,' she said with her mouth full. 'I'm allowed to change my mind.'

'Is that right?'

She leaned back again and grinned. 'That's right. Especially after you've gone to all that trouble to cut everything up so I don't have to struggle with a knife. Anyway, I'm too thin at the moment.'

'You could do with a little more weight,' he said carefully.

She laughed. 'It's OK, I don't have an eating disorder, I've just been off my food since the anaesthetic and I've been walking round Yorkshire with a backpack for the past week or two.'

'Did it work?' he asked, and she could see in his eyes that he understood. For some absurd reason it irritated her.

'It passed the time,' she said shortly, and then had to look away because, again, he understood. 'Um, about me being here,' she said, changing the subject. 'Is it OK if I stay here if I keep out of your way? I can't work, and at least if I'm here I can get to my parents easily to visit them and I can catch up with all my old friends in the area.'

He shrugged. 'Sure. You aren't in my way, and it means I don't have to worry about the dogs.'

The dogs in question wagged their tails hopefully, and he laughed and stood up. 'Sorry, boys, I ate it all. So did Connie. Still, if you ask her nicely she might give you breakfast and take you for walkies.'

Their ears pricked, and they sat up and wagged their tails.

Connie chuckled and pushed back her chair. 'OK, I give in. You go and do surgery, I'll do the dogs. I'll see you later.'

Her father looked well—which, considering he'd just had major surgery, made Connie realise how far downhill he'd slid over the previous couple of years without her really noticing. She felt hugely guilty, and her eyes filled as she walked over to the bed and looked down at him.

His eyes were closed, and as she stood there they flickered open and widened in surprise. 'Connie!' he murmured, and lifted an arm towards her, drawing her down to the edge of the bed. 'What a lovely way to wake up. Your mother said you were coming. Give your old man a hug.'

'Oh, Dad, it is good to see you,' she said emotionally, trying hard not to crush him and hurt his chest. Then she sat back on the edge of the bed and smiled at him again, banishing her sentiment.

'So, you dark horse, how are you then?' she teased.

He smiled tiredly. 'Oh, so-so. Chest hurts. Leg aches. The joker in the next bed keeps trying to make me laugh.'

'Ouch.'

Connie eyed the dressing over the 'zip' of staples running up the centre of his chest, holding the two halves of his breastbone together, and resisted the urge to lift the dressing away and check it out.

'Where's Mum?' she asked, looking round the small ward for any sign of her mother.

'Oh, nipped out to the shops. She'll be back in a

minute. So, where did you get to, you naughty girl? You disappeared.'

She smiled guiltily. 'Sorry. I went to Yorkshire for a few days—I broke my arm and couldn't work, so I thought I might as well make a bit of a holiday of it. I'm sorry, I should have let you know.'

And, please, God, don't let his medical mind kick in and start quizzing me about the fracture.

Fat chance.

'Let me see,' he demanded, and felt her fingers, looking at them, turning her hand over carefully and studying the skin, the cast, the reaction of her hand to his touch. Then he put it down and met her eyes frankly. 'How bad is it?'

'Just a break—'

'Connie? Don't lie to me.'

She sighed. 'It was quite bad,' she said, giving him some of the truth—just enough to keep him quiet and take the edge off his curiosity. 'They had to pin and plate it, but it should recover pretty much—'

'Nerve damage?'

'A little,' she admitted reluctantly. 'Nothing that won't mend. Look, I've brought you some grapes,' she said, changing the subject. 'Where can I put them?'

She fussed about on the locker with the grapes, washed a few at the basin in the corner and shared them with her father.

'So, how's Patrick getting on?' he asked.

'Oh, all right,' she told him, and wondered why she felt a sudden little rush of adrenaline at the sound of his name. How very odd. 'He seems quite happy.' Apart from the bump on the head. Still, he seemed to have recovered and had survived morning surgery and his visits by the time she'd left.

'He's been a huge help. He's stayed with us in the past several times.'

'When you had your heart attacks?'

He coloured slightly. 'Ah. He told you about that.'

'Yes, he did, and you're very naughty not to tell me yourself. How could you keep it from me?' she asked, a little crossly.

'I didn't want to worry you. I knew you'd panic and fuss over me.'

Connie smiled wryly. 'OK, I forgive you. I didn't tell you about my arm for the same reason, so I can understand—'

'Connie! Darling, you came! Let me look at you.'

Oh, here we go, Connie thought. You're too thin, you're too tired, what did you do to your arm?

It was all of that and more, a mother hen clucking over the only surviving member of her brood. Connie tolerated it patiently, glossed over her fracture and changed the subject.

'What did you buy at the shops?'

Her mother laughed. 'Oh, just some fruit and a few pairs of tights. Nothing exciting. So, how are you getting on with Patrick? I hope you won't do anything to upset him.'

The same funny little surge, the same kick of her heart, this time accompanied by another wave of guilt. 'Mum, we've hardly met!' she protested. 'Why would I do anything to upset him?' Apart from clubbing him over the head, of course, for which she still felt racked with remorse. That and half accusing him of pinching the silver. She changed the subject again swiftly.

'Tell me all about this op, then, you two. When was it, how did it go, when are you coming home? I want all the answers.'

'They say two weeks,' her father said, 'but I can't imagine I'll feel up to it. Still, it's early days. I only had the op on Wednesday, so it's a week tomorrow, and I must say I feel a darned sight better now than I did five or six days ago!'

'I'm sure,' Connie murmured, wondering what it was about families that fostered such huge feelings of guilt and responsibility.

Not that it would have made any difference at all to the surgeon's skill if she'd been around, but she just felt as if she'd abandoned him. Heavens, if she ever got the chance to find out, she was sure she'd be a dreadfully clucky mother! Perhaps it was just as well there was nothing on the cards in that direction.

Inexplicably she thought of Patrick, and a whole row of little Patricks with dark hair and grey eyes and cheeky smiles, and something inside her ached in the most curious way.

It must be your age, she told herself, and tried to pay attention to what her father was saying about his operation.

'Thank you, Doctor.'

'You're welcome.' Patrick smiled and said goodbye to his last patient, then stood up and stretched. It was ten past six—pretty good going, really, considering the inauspicious start to the day. He gingerly explored the bump on his head, wincing as he pressed a little too hard, but it was early days. At least his headache had worn off.

There was a light tap on the door and Jan, the cheerful, middle-aged senior receptionist, popped her head round it. 'Would you mind doing a visit, Dr Durrant? A little boy with tummy ache. He's been sick and he's a bit hot. It's just in the village. I know you're not on call but it sounded quite urgent.'

Patrick nodded. 'Sure. They can't get in, I take it?'

'I think he's being quite sick. She didn't like to move him.'

'OK, I'll go. Got the notes?'

Jan smiled and handed them to him, together with the directions. 'Here you are, you can't miss it. Burnt House Farm. Tim Roberts.'

It was only five minutes away in the car, and when he arrived and saw the child Patrick was profoundly grateful that he'd finished so promptly and that he hadn't had far to come, because the child was very ill indeed. Mrs Roberts ushered him into the sitting room. 'Tim? The doctor's here, darling,' she said softly.

He didn't move. Patrick sat carefully on the edge of the sofa beside the boy and studied him. He was pale, sweaty, his eyes closed, and he was breathing very carefully. Every now and then he gave a little grunt, and Patrick found his pulse was rapid and thready.

'Tim, can you tell me where you hurt?' Patrick said, but the boy just moaned softly. No help there, then. He looked up at the mother. 'When did he start feeling ill?'

'Yesterday? Maybe even the night before. He didn't eat much supper, and yesterday he said he had a bit of tummy ache and he felt sick. Then today he seemed to go suddenly downhill after lunch, and now he looks awful.'

He certainly did. Patrick turned back the covers and gently eased down the boy's pyjama trousers so he could see his abdomen. It was rigid, held motionless by the tension of the muscles, and there was an area of warmth and a slight reddening down on the right hand side.

'Is it appendicitis?' the mother asked anxiously.

'Possibly. I'm just going to have a little listen to your tummy, Tim.' Patrick took out his stethoscope and checked for bowel sounds, but there were none. He pursed his lips and folded the instrument up again, covering the child lightly.

'Is he usually brave?'

'Oh, yes,' Mrs Roberts said ruefully. 'He broke his arm once and didn't make a murmur. If it hadn't have been for the funny angle, we wouldn't have known.'

Patrick nodded and stood up, motioning her out of the room and out of earshot. 'I think he might have a burst appendix,' he said softly. 'I want him into hospital as fast as possible, just in case I'm wrong and it hasn't gone yet. Do you have a phone so I can ring for an ambulance?'

Mrs Roberts pressed her hand against her chest and swallowed convulsively. 'Burst— Oh, my. Um. Phone. Yes, of course. Can I go with him?'

'Sure. Let me ring the hospital as well and tell them you're on the way, and they'll sort out a bed for you. Have you got any other children to make arrangements for?'

She shook her head numbly. 'No. Only my husband—he'll be in soon. He's out feeding the pigs at the moment. I'd better leave him a note.'

She left Patrick phoning and went to pack some things, and when he'd made the calls he went back and set up an IV line, running in saline to boost the boy's flagging circulation. He was shocked, and Patrick was glad it had happened during the day and not at night, because by the morning the child might have been dead. These little toughies were often the hardest to look after, he thought, glad that the boy was now stable and seemed not to be deteriorating any further.

He waited till the ambulance came, then left at the same time as it did to go back to the surgery. A taxi turned into the drive just ahead of him and Connie got out, paid the taxi driver and then turned to him with a smile as he locked his car.

'Hi. How are you feeling?'

'Better, thank you. You can relax, Connie, I haven't called the police.'

She gave a wry grin. 'Just checking. Mum and Dad send their love and want to know if we're getting on all right and if you're coping. I told them not to worry.'

'How does he look?'

'Good. He looks better than he's looked for ages. I can't believe I didn't pick up on it.'

She sounded so disgusted with herself that Patrick felt sorry for her. 'Don't flagellate yourself,' he advised. 'Have you eaten?'

She shook her head, sending the fine strands of gold-red hair flying in the evening sun. 'No. Why?'

'Because I'm starved and there's nothing but dog food in the house. Fancy a Chinese?'

'Only if you let me treat you.'

'Why should I do that?'

'Because I tried to kill you?' she suggested with a rueful look.

'Oh, that. Tell you what, we'll go halves. You can treat me, and I'll treat you. Deal?'

She smiled, a warm, pretty, sexy smile that lit up her face and made his breath jam in his throat. 'Deal,' she agreed softly, and he wondered if he'd get through the meal without choking or making a complete ass of himself.

Just then it seemed highly unlikely!

Patrick was a wonderful dinner companion. Charming, witty, attentive—it was so long since she'd been exposed to the full force of an attractive man that Connie felt a little stunned.

She also felt full, and belatedly realised that he'd kept her mind occupied so that she'd eat—and he'd sneaked food onto her plate over and over again while she'd been distracted by his charm and wit.

How like a man to trick her. How could she not have noticed what was going on? She must be going senile.

They split the bill fifty-fifty, although she was sure she'd eaten more than her share, and on the way back she reclined her seat, patted her distended stomach and gave him a jaundiced look. 'You conned me into eating,' she said comfortably, without any real rancour.

He shot her a grin. 'You noticed.'

'Only when it was too late. I shall probably be sick.'

He chuckled. 'I doubt it. By the way, remind me to phone the hospital. I admitted a young boy just after surgery with a query burst appendix and peritonitis— I'd like to find out how he's doing.'

'Who is it?' Connie asked, mildly curious. She knew most of the people in the village, and probably knew the parents.

'Tim Roberts—Burnt House Farm.'

She sat bolt upright. 'Tim? He's my godson!'

Patrick shot her an apologetic look. 'Ah. Sorry. I think he'll be OK. He's a toughie.'

'He certainly is. He broke his arm last year and Dad couldn't believe how little fuss he made. I'd better talk to them. Did Jackie seem all right?'

'His mother? Fine. A bit shocked, but all right, really. She's gone in with him.'

She ran through her A and E training in her head. 'Did you give him IV fluids?'

'Yes, of course. There wasn't time to do anything else. The ambulance came very quickly from the outstation. I didn't have time to blink.'

He swung into the drive and parked the car, and by the time Connie had struggled to undo her seat belt with the wrong hand he'd come round and opened her door for her.

'I'm not a cripple,' she said a little shortly, and he tutted and closed the door after her, locking the car with the remote.

'I thought eating was supposed to improve your temper,' he mused, ushering her to the kitchen door and letting them both in. The dogs bounced around and greeted them cheerfully, and he flicked on the lights, put on the kettle and met Connie's eyes with a steady, searching look.

'Tea?'

'I can make it.'

'I don't doubt it. However, I was offering. Don't get so defensive that you misread anything anyone does for you as patronage,' he warned. 'One day you might need help, and there'll be nobody there for you if you've driven them all away.'

Connie looked down, a heavy sigh escaping before she could stop it. 'I'm sorry,' she said tiredly. 'I was just irritated because I couldn't do the seat belt. I think

I'll go up to bed. Last night was a bit hectic. Are you OK to do the dogs and lock up?'

'I think I'll manage,' he said drily. 'Want me to bring you a hot milky drink?'

She gave him a filthy look. 'I haven't had a hot milky drink since I was about eight.'

He grinned. 'Brandy, then?'

Connie relented and smiled. 'I'm sorry—again. No, I don't want a brandy. I really am tired.'

He nodded. 'OK. I'll see you in the morning. Sleep well, Connie.'

She went upstairs and sat down on the edge of her bed, running back over the evening in her mind. She heard Patrick on the phone, and went back out onto the landing just as he came up.

'Did you just ring about Tim?' she asked, appalled that she could have forgotten him.

'Yes—he's through surgery. It *had* burst, but they've cleaned him up and they're blasting him with antibiotics. I was just coming up to tell you.'

'Oh. Right. Thanks.'

She hesitated, hovering on the landing just feet from him, her heart pounding and her mind a blank.

He almost stepped towards her. She saw him hesitate, saw something flicker in his eyes and then he smiled, a little, tiny half-smile. 'Goodnight, Connie,' he murmured, and, turning on his heel, he ran lightly back downstairs. She heard the kitchen door shut with a soft click, and then it was quiet.

She went to bed, curled up under the quilt and wondered why she felt so alone tonight, when she'd been alone at night for her entire life. Well, almost, she corrected, remembering that brief fling years before when she'd had the time.

Perhaps she ought to get the dogs to come and sleep on her bed, but they were in the kitchen and so was Patrick, and there was no way she was going down there in the long T-shirt that she used as a nightie and admitting that she needed company!

She thumped the pillow and tried to get comfortable, but her arm was aching and her fingers tingled and itched, and she wanted to scream.

She heard Patrick come up to bed, and to her surprise he went into the spare room next to hers, and not through into the locum's room over the surgery in the other wing of the house.

How odd. The locums always slept over the surgery. She wondered why Patrick didn't, and hard on the heels of the thought was another one, much more disturbing.

He was just on the other side of the wall. She heard the jingle of keys on a hard surface, and the thud of a shoe falling. She held her breath, and then giggled. The saying 'waiting for the other shoe to drop' suddenly made sense. She heard a soft thud, and then the creak of the floorboards and the squeak of the wardrobe door. Hanging up his clothes?

Oh, Lord. The image of him that morning in the bathroom returned to haunt her, and she wondered why it was now, when she had nothing to offer and more worries than she could shake a stick at, that she suddenly had to fall for a man she had to share a house with for the next few weeks!

Well, too bad. She was an adult, with self-control and self-discipline. So he was attractive. So what? Lots of men were attractive. That didn't mean she had to lose sleep over them, did it?

Of course not!

*   *   *

Patrick propped himself up against the headboard, folded his arms behind his head and tried not to think about Connie tucked up in bed on the other side of the wall. She was too thin, too tiny and fragile and delicate for his taste. He preferred a woman with a bit of meat on her, something to hold onto, something soft and warm and enveloping, not a scraggy child-woman with huge haunted eyes and jeans he was jealous of.

Unbidden, he thought of the way he'd first seen her, in that short T-shirt and those ridiculous knickers, with that soft, vulnerable expanse of skin between the two, and he groaned.

How could he want her? She was so tiny, so frail...

He laughed softly. Frail? She'd nearly killed him with the cricket bat! She'd just been backpacking round Yorkshire with a broken arm. She might be small, she might have slight bones, but frail she was not.

And despite all his protests about liking his women well covered, his body knew it was a lie.

Connie Wright was a very attractive young woman, and whatever garbage he told himself, he wanted her.

Well, tough. He had more going on in his life than Connie realised, and there was no way he was going to allow a little lust to distract him and complicate things further.

He switched off the light, curled onto his side and shut his eyes.

It wasn't that easy. As he drifted off, Connie was there, dancing in front of his eyes in nothing but kitten-print knickers and the sexiest smile he'd ever seen...

CHAPTER THREE

CONNIE'S arm hurt.

It didn't matter which way she lay, how she propped it up, what she did with it. It ached, with a deep and heavy ache that made her want to cry with frustration.

She slipped out of bed, tiptoed downstairs and went through to the surgery. Perhaps there were some strong painkillers out on the shelves in the dispensary. She flicked on the lights, deplored her father's apparently unsystematic retrieval system and searched the shelves fruitlessly for something to send her off to sleep.

'Connie?'

Patrick spoke softly, but he may as well have let off a gun behind her for all the difference it made. She jumped about a foot, spun round with her hand over her heart and glared at him.

'Are you trying to terrify the life out of me?' she demanded, sagging back against the wall.

He grinned. 'Sorry. Arm hurting?'

She sighed and stabbed her left hand through her already disordered hair. 'You might say that. I just can't get comfortable.'

'Let me look at it.'

She resisted the urge to hide it behind her back. 'Why? I know what I need.'

'Yes—a prescription-only medicine, nicked from the shelves of my dispensary. Sorry, Connie, if you want painkillers other than aspirin or paracetamol, you'll have to let me look at you.'

She knew he was right, but she felt very naked—again—and hideously disadvantaged. She shoved her arm out in front of her ungraciously and tapped her foot. 'Here it is—look, if you must. I was going to tell you what I'd taken. I just didn't want to disturb you.'

'I don't mind,' he said softly, and, amazingly, she believed him. She instantly felt guilty for being so ungracious, but it was too late to take it back. Instead, she submitted to his careful and thorough examination.

His hand was warm and gentle, covering her fingers, turning her arm over, flexing the finger joints, feeling for swelling or poor circulation.

'The cast isn't too tight or anything,' she told him.

'I'm just looking to see if there's a problem brewing—maybe with the pins or plates. Has it hurt in the past, or is this new?'

Connie shifted against the wall, closing her eyes and resigning herself to a full-blooded interrogation as well. 'It's hurt ever since it was done. I think it's just all the damage. I had a new cast two weeks ago to see if that helped, but it didn't really.'

'How did the arm look, then?'

Disfigured, she thought, but that was a subjective assessment, not a medical one. 'OK.'

'Incisions healed all right?'

She nodded. 'The stitches have been out for a month or more.'

'And did they X-ray you when they changed the cast?'

'Yes—look, Patrick, this is pointless. The damn thing just hurts, OK? I need some DF118s or something like that.'

His fingers curled around hers, squeezing gently, warm and firm and comforting. 'Can you feel that?'

All the way through me, she could have said, but she managed to restrain herself. 'Yes, of course.'

'And this?'

She looked down, to see him pressing on her index finger with his nail. Just lightly, but she couldn't feel it at all. She swallowed and shook her head. 'No,' she said, and her voice sounded scratchy. Damn.

He nodded and let go, and she felt a huge sense of loss as he broke the contact. 'I'll give you something to take the pain away and help you sleep, then in the morning I think you should ring the consultant and maybe go back and see him.'

'Her—and I know what she'd say.'

'You're doing too much and should have it in a sling and rest it for a week or so?'

Her smile was wry and reluctant, but his eyes crinkled in response and he slipped his arm round her shoulders and hugged her gently.

'Go on through to the kitchen and have a hot drink, and I'll write you out a script and bring it in.'

She nodded and went back into the house, but instead of going into the kitchen she went upstairs and dug out an old towelling robe. If she was going to have to sit in the kitchen with Patrick and sip cocoa, she was wearing more than a T-shirt to do it!

Patrick was in the kitchen when Connie got back down there, pan in one hand, a bottle of milk in the other, and a packet of pills was sitting in the middle of the kitchen table for her. He gestured to the milk. 'Hot chocolate or malt?'

'Black coffee.'

He snorted and poured the milk into the pan. 'Sorry. Hot milk contains calcium which boosts the production of the chemicals that promote sleep. So it's hot milk or hot milk, basically. And no, you aren't having coffee in it.'

She grinned in defeat and dropped into a chair, her hand falling onto Toby's shaggy head and fondling it automatically. 'Hot chocolate, then, if you're going to bully me.'

'I am.'

Rolo came up on the other side, his lovely golden head shoving against the cast and pleading for attention. She tried to stroke him, but her arm was tired and uncooperative and she just thumped him over the head with the cast instead.

He sighed and lay down, his head heavy on her foot, and shut his eyes. Toby leaned against her, his chin on her knee, and she pulled his ears gently and wondered what she'd done to earn their devotion.

'Here you go—one hot chocolate. Don't burn your mouth.'

'I'm not six,' she said ungraciously, and then smiled to soften it. 'Thanks, Patrick,' she added.

'You're welcome.' He sat down opposite her and pushed the pills across the table to her. 'Take two of these with it.'

She nodded, but was defeated first by the cardboard box and then by the blister pack. Frustrated, irritated beyond reason and almost in tears, she threw the packet down with a growl of anger and looked away.

'Here.'

She looked back, to see Patrick holding out his hand with two pills in the palm of it. He had his patient, get-it-out-of-your-system look on, and immediately she felt ashamed. 'I'm sorry.' She sighed. 'It's just—getting to me.'

'I can imagine. Don't apologise. Just take the pills,

drink the drink and go back to bed with a book. You'll be asleep in no time.'

She snorted. 'I wouldn't bet on it. I haven't been able to sleep for weeks, so I don't imagine you'll be able to work a miracle with your hot milk and happy pills.'

He chuckled. 'It's worth a try. What do you want me to do, read you a bedtime story?'

Make love to me, she nearly said, and then felt herself colour. She looked down hastily and prodded the froth on her drink. 'I think I can manage to read my own bedtime story,' she said drily, to cover her confusion. She didn't know him, for heaven's sake! She had absolutely never felt like this! She was so circumspect it was ridiculous. Even her parents worried that she didn't get out enough. And yet here she was, all ready to throw herself headlong at Patrick just because he had passable looks and was a captive audience!

'I think I'll take this upstairs, actually,' she said, and, grabbing the drink, she fled for the relative sanctuary of her bedroom. At least there he wouldn't be able to read her thoughts quite so easily!

She heard him come up a few minutes later and hesitate at her door. She held her breath, hoping—what? That he would come in? Or not?

He didn't, and she suppressed a pang of disappointment. She turned her attention back to her book, and after a few more minutes she found her eyelids drooping. His wretched hot milk gimmick was working, she thought with wry disgust, and putting out the light, she snuggled down and drifted off to sleep.

For the next couple of days Connie felt as if she were in limbo. She visited her father again, walked the dogs, spent some time with young Tim Roberts, her godson, who was recovering slowly from his burst appendix and subsequent peritonitis, and found herself going quietly nuts.

On Friday, she went into the surgery during the morning rush-hour, as her father called it, and perched on a stool in Reception and got in the way.

'Connie, as you're sitting there, you couldn't get me out Mrs Grieves's notes, could you?' Jan asked. 'Holly Cottage.'

'Sure.' She swivelled round, pulled out the wide drawer with the Gs, found the right packet and replaced it with a brightly coloured marker, to make it easier putting them back. Simple system, she thought, but effective. Her father was full of clever ideas. 'Here.'

'Thanks—oh, and these could go away. They're last night's, and I haven't had time to deal with them. We've been so busy with Sally off this week. It's a good job Tanya could get in this morning or we would have been really stuck without a dispenser. It's always hell before a weekend.'

Connie sat back and gave an exaggerated sigh. 'You should have said something, Jan! I've been sitting in there keeping out of the way twiddling my thumbs! I'm so bored I can't tell you! You want help, you've got help. Tell me what to do.'

Jan smiled. 'I just did. And when you've done that, you could always put the kettle on. Dr Durrant usually has a cup of coffee before he goes out on his calls, and we could all do with one.'

Filing and coffee. Still, it beats cleaning the bathroom with my left hand, she thought, and slotted the notes away. In fact, there was another emergency tacked on to the end of surgery, so she drank her coffee, filed the earlier notes from that morning, which Patrick had brought through, and by the time he was going out on his calls, they were up to date.

'I don't suppose you want company on your travels, do you?' she asked wistfully.

He grinned. 'Time hanging on your hands? Actually, I wouldn't mind. I still get a bit lost sometimes. You can map-read for me.'

'Only if you promise not to yell,' she warned, and he grinned again.

'I promise. Just don't do anything stupid.'

She snorted and slid off the stool. 'Are you OK if I go out with him, Jan?'

The receptionist nodded. 'Fine. Tanya's nearly done, and I've just got the routine stuff to do. I could do with a hand this afternoon, though, if you've got time. There's an antenatal clinic and it's a bit hectic. If you did nothing else you could entertain the children while the mums are seen.'

Connie screwed up her nose and laughed. 'Babysitting now! OK, I'll see you later.'

'Are you sure?'

She grinned. 'It's fine. I love babies. That's why I'm a paediatrician.'

'Connie, are you coming?' Patrick asked, holding the door and glancing at his watch. She pulled a face at Jan, waggled her fingers and trotted obediently after him.

'Where are we going first?' she asked as they set off.

'Shrubbery Farm. Old Mrs Pike's had a fall. They've put her in bed but she's complaining her hip hurts.'

'Oh, dear.'

'Quite. We'll see if it's broken when we get there.'

'No, I meant, oh, dear, Mrs Pike. She's really difficult. She's deaf as a post, won't take advice, complains about the slightest thing and nothing's ever good enough.'

He shot her a wry smile. 'Thanks for the warning. We'll see what happens.'

Mrs Pike's daughter-in-law opened the door to them, and ushered them through to the downstairs sitting room their patient used as a bedroom. She was lying on her pillows, arms folded primly across her middle, and she glowered at them. 'Took your time.' That was her first remark, and Patrick seemed to hold his breath.

'Sorry, Mrs Pike, I was held up at the surgery,' he said, good and loud so she could hear. 'You remember Dr Wright's daughter? She's a doctor herself now— she's helping me today, making sure I don't get lost.'

Mrs Pike looked across at Connie and sniffed. 'Aren't you married yet, girl? Time you settled down instead of running around pretending to be a doctor. No job for a woman. What've you done to your arm?'

'I fell,' she yelled. 'It's fine. That's why I'm here. I gather you've done the same.'

'Nothing wrong with my arm.'

'I meant, you fell,' Connie explained.

'Oh, yes. Hurt my hip.' She swivelled her gimlet eyes to Patrick. 'Suppose you're going to try and tell me it's broken, but I know it isn't because I can walk on it. Hurts like the devil, though. Need something nice and strong to take away the pain.'

'Let me just have a look,' Patrick said soothingly,

and then had to repeat it because he was too soothing and she didn't hear.

Connie watched from a safe distance for the sake of her ears, while Patrick and Mrs Pike argued about the fact that her hip was indeed broken, that the broken ends of the neck of the femur had been driven together and thus impacted by the fall, and, yes, she would have to go to hospital although she might not need an operation, and, no, her daughter-in-law couldn't possibly manage to look after her properly and the physio couldn't come daily to see her and the district nurse had too much to do to come three times a day to someone who needed hospitalisation!

Connie stifled a smile and exchanged speaking glances with the daughter-in-law, who was clearly looking forward to a few quiet days without her husband's troublesome mother.

'I don't want to go,' Mrs Pike said, as if that made it unnecessary, and Patrick covered her up again, put his stethoscope back in his bag and picked it up.

'All right,' he yelled, smiling tolerantly. 'You stay here, then, but I have to warn you you'll probably be crippled and never be able to get out of bed again. You might get awfully sick of these four walls, but if that's the way you want it, Mrs Pike, I can't admit you against your will. Nor can I give you the stronger painkillers without proper supervision, but there you go. I'll pop in tomorrow. Have a good night.'

And he headed for the door, leaving Connie and the younger Mrs Pike open-mouthed.

'Just a minute,' the old dragon called.

He paused and looked over his shoulder. 'Yes?'

'Crippled?'

'Oh, undoubtedly. And in permanent pain.'

She sniffed. 'Better go, then. Have you called the ambulance?'

'No.'

'Well, why ever not, if I've got not choice? You should have said I've got no choice!'

'Thought I did,' he murmured softly, and winked at Connie. 'We'll phone an ambulance now.'

'Next?'

'New mum just come home from the maternity unit. You'll like this one.'

Connie chuckled. 'I liked the last one. Poor Mrs Pike. That was a mean trick.'

He looked at her. 'It was no trick, Connie. I have no right to admit her against her will unless I consider she's not in sound mind and can't make a judgement. If she hadn't stopped me, I would have gone and called in tomorrow and had another go.'

'But she did stop you.'

'Thank God, because she's the sort of person who'd sue if she refused treatment and then suffered as a result. I'm glad you warned me.'

She chuckled again. 'My pleasure. Right, who's the new mum?'

'Jennie Defoe. I know the way to her house.'

Connie racked her brains. 'Defoe—are they new to the village?'

'Could be. He's Michael Morgan's farm manager. Nice couple—about our age.'

They pulled up outside the Defoes' house, and as soon as the girl opened the door, Connie recognised her. 'Jenny Walker!' she said in delight. 'Well, hi!'

'Connie! What are you doing here?'

'Helping me find places,' Patrick explained, but his

explanation was superfluous. Connie was towed away by her old school friend, and within moments was cuddling the new baby and admiring it.

Patrick asked questions and flicked through the chart, prodded Jennie's abdomen and declared that she was doing well, then stole the baby from Connie and cuddled it for a minute before they set off.

'Gorgeous baby,' Connie said with a sigh as they got back into the car.

'Isn't he?'

There was something about his voice that caught Connie's attention, and she looked up and saw an expression of deep and aching sadness on his face.

At least, she thought she did, but it was gone in less than a second so that she wondered if she'd imagined it. Then he was all brisk business again, asking for directions to the next call.

It was obscure enough to demand Connie's attention, and she managed to find the way without getting lost once, to her amazement. And then, of course, the moment was long gone and she couldn't ask—what?

Whatever could she have asked that could have explained the sadness on his face? 'Have you lost a child?' 'Are you divorced?' 'Are you sterile?'

Hardly.

They went back to the surgery, and she threw together some cheese and biscuits before the antenatal clinic in the afternoon, and she wondered if she'd ever know.

Patrick glanced through the stack of notes before the start of his antenatal clinic, and hesitated at Mrs Bailey's. She'd had polyhydramnios, an excess of amniotic fluid, and he'd sent her to the consultant for further investigation.

He looked through her notes, but there was no consultant's letter, and, in fact, he didn't think she was due to see him again yet so he wondered what had prompted her visit.

He found out when her turn came. She was huge. Not just the ponderous fullness of late pregnancy—indeed, her pregnancy wasn't that far advanced—but the bloated, painfully distended fullness of a rapidly worsening condition.

She sank down onto the chair in relief, sitting with her knees apart and leaning back simply to accommodate the 'bump'.

'Hello, Mrs Bailey. You look as if you're struggling,' he said gently.

She shook her head in despair. 'I am. I've been to see the consultant, and had a scan yesterday, and he told me there's something wrong with the baby—'

She broke off, clearly upset, and he gave her a tissue and waited for a moment for her to go on.

'Did he suggest what it might be?' he asked, hoping it wasn't that the baby was anencephalic—without proper brain development—but that it was a more correctable condition like oesophageal atresia.

It was. 'He said the baby's oesophagus hadn't developed properly, that it ended in a blind sac and so the baby wasn't able to swallow. I don't really understand why that should make me swell up like this, though. He said something about the baby drinking it, but where does it go?'

'Didn't he explain it to you?'

She shrugged. 'A little, but the clinic was bursting at the seams, he seemed a bit distracted, and to be honest, I was so shell-shocked I didn't really take it all in.'

Patrick nodded. 'OK. Right, well, let's start with the mechanics of pregnancy. In the last part, the phase you're just entering, the baby starts to drink and pee, but obviously that isn't going to get rid of the fluid. However, the excess fluid is removed from the baby's circulation via the placenta, and so if the baby isn't able to swallow and the placenta can't remove the fluid, then it just builds up.'

'But why? I thought there was however much there was and that was it.'

Patrick shook his head. 'No. The amniotic membrane—the caul that surrounds the baby—produces a fresh supply all the time, so that it's continuously replaced. In your case, though, it's just making it and it isn't being removed, so you just get more and more. Only the pressure of your distended uterus will prevent any more being made.'

She gave a wry smile. 'Is that why I haven't exploded yet?'

'Probably,' he said with a chuckle. 'Anyway, in a way it's good news, because at least we now know what's wrong with the baby. Did he give you a letter to give me?'

'No. He said he'd be writing, but I couldn't wait to see you, I was so worried. He said something about an operation when it's born—'

Again she broke off, obviously upset at the thought of her tiny baby needing major surgery so early in its life. I need to reassure her, Patrick thought, and then through the door he heard Connie's laugh as she played with the children in the waiting room.

'Excuse me a moment, would you?' he said, and

stuck his head round the door. 'Connie? Got a minute?'

She stood up and came over, a curious expression on her face. 'Yes?'

'Oesophageal atresia?'

She nodded. 'I wondered. Want me to have a word about the operation? I've done it a few times.'

He sighed with relief. 'Would you? I think Mrs Bailey would be relieved.'

'Sure.'

'How about using the counselling room upstairs?'

She shook her head. 'The sofa's low and the stairs are a pain. We'll go in the kitchen.' She smiled at the patient and held out her hand. 'Mrs Bailey? I'm Connie Wright, Dr Wright's daughter. I'm a paediatric surgeon. I can tell you all about it. Shall we go and have a cuppa?'

Patrick watched them go, Mrs Bailey and a different Connie, fired with an enthusiasm and professional manner that he hadn't seen in her before, and his heart ached for what she'd lost and what the field of paediatric neonatal surgery would be denied, all because of a stupid, unnecessary fall.

'So,' Connie said, struggling with her left hand to draw the anatomy of a baby, 'what we do is open the chest, join the ends of the oesophagus, close any connection between the oesophagus and the windpipe and sew the baby up again.'

'You make it sound so straightforward and easy.'

'Well, I don't know about easy...' Connie chuckled, '...but it's usually very straightforward, and if there are no other complications, the baby then goes on to lead a perfectly normal life.'

'Except for the scar.'

'It fades,' she assured the woman. 'It really does almost disappear as they grow up. It's not like the scar you get from heart surgery as an adult, I promise you, and even if it was, isn't it better than dying?'

'Oh, yes,' Mrs Bailey said fervently. 'I didn't mean that. I just thought, if it's a girl—well, it would be a shame.'

'It's always a shame. It's a shame it's had to happen, but at least it's happened now when we can do something about it and not a hundred years ago.'

Mrs Bailey nodded and smiled. 'I suppose you're right. So, will I have to go on like this for another six weeks?'

Connie looked at the hugely distended bump and wondered how she could bear it at all. 'No,' she assured her. 'What the consultant will do, I imagine, is strike a balance. He'll probably leave you for as long as possible, making sure that the pressure isn't affecting the baby, and then once he feels the baby's big enough, he'll probably try drawing off some of the fluid to reduce the pressure.'

'Like amniocentesis?'

Connie nodded. 'Exactly, only they take off rather more fluid! It usually only helps for a little while, but they can do it more than once if necessary, although it will probably trigger labour in some women. At that point they'll probably induce you anyway—wearing wellies!'

Mrs Bailey laughed. 'I should imagine they'd need to! I feel like a water bomb at the moment. I just hope I don't fall over. I'll probably burst!'

Connie joined in her laughter, then patted her hand. 'Are you feeling better about it now? A bit happier?'

'Oh, yes. Thank you so much. It really has helped.'

'Good. And you will keep in touch with us, won't you? If you're at all worried, you must ring or come straight back, OK? Don't worry about wasting Dr Durrant's time—that's what he's here for. All right?'

The patient nodded, relief clear in her gentle hazel eyes, and Connie wished she could be the one doing the operation. Still, it was just a matter of time. Once the nerves healed, she could go back and get on with her life, instead of living in this empty limbo.

She showed the patient out and went back to her little charges, entertaining them while their mothers were in with Patrick or the nurse, and wondered if any more interesting cases would come in or if it would be all plain sailing.

Not that she would wish complications on any of them—it had just been interesting to talk to Mrs Bailey.

'It's mine!'

'No, mine! Mummy!'

She turned her attention back to the children. 'Shall we see what else is in here? Oh, look at this lovely tractor!'

Patrick came out of his surgery half an hour later to find Connie sitting on the floor, chucking toys back in the box.

'OK?' he asked, hunkering down beside her and helping to clear the toys.

She nodded, her hair falling over her face like a fine golden veil. He had an insane urge to tuck it back behind her ears, but before he could her hand was there, anchoring the soft strands firmly. She used her left hand, he noticed, even though it was the right side. Oh, dear.

'How did you get on with Mrs Bailey?' he asked, wanting to see that other Connie again, but she just shrugged.

'OK. I told her what happens, and she seemed to understand. She's not unintelligent. I think she's feeling a lot happier now, anyway.'

He nodded. 'Thanks. And thanks for helping with this lot, as well.'

She laughed. 'My pleasure, but you can give me neonates instead any day—toddlers can be the giddy limit!'

That sounded a bit too familiar. He straightened up. 'So they say,' he murmured, and stuck his head through the hatch into the office. 'OK, ladies?'

'Fine. Want a cup of tea?'

'Love one. I could drink a desert dry. I don't suppose we've got any cake?'

Jan smiled. 'How did I know you'd say that?' she teased, and brandished a cake tin. 'I made one of my honey cakes for us last night.'

Patrick grinned. 'Jan, you're a saviour. Connie, are you having cake?'

'Sounds good,' she said, getting to her feet and dusting off her knees. 'In fact, after that lot, it sounds wonderful! Remind me never to have a toddler!'

They all laughed. 'What are you going to do if you have a baby?' Jan asked practically.

'Send it to boarding school at one,' Connie said bluntly. 'I might have it back at ten.'

Jan and Tanya roared with laughter. 'That's when the trouble starts!' Tanya said.

Patrick said nothing. There was nothing to say—not

to this light-hearted lot. He took his tea and cake and went back to his room to finish working on the notes.

Patrick was out that night on call, and Connie was just curling up in front of the television when a car pulled up on the drive. The dogs whined, and she shut them in the sitting room and went to the door. The outside light had come on automatically, and she opened the door to reveal a long, sleek car, its engine running and lights still on. The driver's door opened and a leggy, curvaceous blonde stepped out without cutting the engine. She glanced at Connie dismissively, opened the back door and beckoned to a child.

He slid out, standing uncertainly to one side. Wide, solemn grey eyes framed by dark lashes studied Connie seriously from a pale, fine-boned little face. Floppy fair hair tipped down over his forehead, and ears like little pink shells stuck out sideways from his head. He looked as if he would break at any minute.

He was about four, Connie guessed, and about as different from the happy, laughing children she'd been entertaining all afternoon as it was possible to get.

The woman pulled a case off the back seat, pushed the child towards Connie and spoke at last.

'Patrick is here, I take it?'

'He's out on call. Can I help you?'

Cold eyes scanned her. 'Are you the latest? Good luck to you. Take my advice and don't get pregnant. Patrick's funny about abortion.'

She thrust the child towards Connie again. 'He wanted him, he can have him. My nanny's left me, I'm off to Antigua and I can't possibly take him. Anyway, I imagine it's what Patrick will want. I only went for custody to annoy him, but it's got boring.'

Finally, when Connie couldn't believe she could get any worse, she bent down and gazed sternly at the little lad. 'Do try and be good, Edward. I really can't have you back if you upset him, you know. It just doesn't work, not with Ron.'

She straightened up and looked Connie in the eye. 'I'll be back home in about six weeks or so. I'll arrange for the rest of his stuff to be shipped up then. Tell Patrick I hope they'll be very happy together.'

And she turned on her heel and left, stepping back into the car and swishing off the drive without another word or a backward glance.

CHAPTER FOUR

CONNIE stood stunned for a moment, then crouched down next to the child. 'Edward?' she said gently.

He looked at her again, those solemn, wary eyes, so like Patrick's, taking it all in. Connie could have wept for him. 'Shall we go in? Daddy's out at the moment, but he'll be back soon. Have you had supper?'

He nodded. 'Yes, thank you,' he said quietly.

So polite, so reserved—so unnatural.

'Well, how about a drink? Would you like a drink?'

He nodded again, and she picked up the case, laid a gentle hand on his shoulder and led him inside. He was going to have to sleep somewhere, of course, but where?

There was only her parents' bedroom, or Anthony's.

Which would, of course, be perfect. She took Edward into the sitting room, introduced him to the dogs who wagged happily at him but didn't jump up or scare him, and then she left him with a silly game show on the television and went to find a drink.

He was still sitting motionless on the edge of the sofa when she brought back a glass of orange juice, and she put it on the coffee-table. 'Here, Edward. Your drink. I'm just going to go and sort out your bedroom for you and run you a bath, OK?'

He nodded, his eyes unblinking, and she went upstairs shaking her head in disbelief. She couldn't credit the woman, speaking about the child like that when he was right under her nose!

'Wicked, wicked witch,' she muttered, and stomped into Anthony's room, flicking on the light.

Memories flooded her. She remembered when he'd found the rusty old propeller on the wall, out in the fields behind the house, and when he'd won the canoeing race with the paddle on the other wall.

His teddy sat on the pillow, and a row of Beatrix Potter and Enid Blyton books graced the bookshelves, cheek by jowl with mystery writers, political thrillers and medical texts.

It was a real boy's room, she thought fondly, and then took down the girly calendar off the back of the door. There was another picture inside the wardrobe, used as a dartboard with a pert, dark nipple as the bull's eye, and she took that down, too.

Better. She made up the bed quickly, ran a bath and went back down.

He was still there, in the same place, but the dogs had bracketed his legs and he was fondling their ears. He jumped guiltily as she went in, folding his hands in his lap as if he was afraid to be caught touching the dogs.

Deliberately, she reached down and patted each one, then looked at the glass. It was empty, drained and put back in exactly the same spot.

'Bath?' she suggested, and he stood up.

'OK.'

She had an idea, and slipped through to the surgery, bringing back the box of toys. There was a yellow plastic duck in there, and she pulled it out victoriously. 'There! Now you'll have company in the water. Come on.'

Bathtime was quiet. She gave up trying to entertain him, and instead concentrated on washing him and getting him into the expensive but uncomfortable looking pyjamas that were in the case. That in itself was hard enough with only one hand.

Once he was dressed in his nightclothes, they went downstairs and had a milky drink together, Connie mindful of Patrick's remedy for her sleepless night and wondering how the little lad could possibly sleep after the awful scene with his mother.

Maybe he was used to her, poor child. How dreadful, to be used to that! He stifled a little yawn, and Connie put down her mug. 'Time for bed, I think, don't you?'

'Will Daddy be long?' he asked, the first unsolicited remark he'd made, and she was sorry to have to give him the wrong answer.

'I'm afraid so,' she said. 'He won't be back until after midnight—he's on call at the night surgery.'

'Can I stay up?' he asked, and suppressed another yawn.

Connie debated, but then shook her head. 'No, I don't think so. It'll be much too late. I'll send him in to you when he comes back, I promise.'

His face remained impassive. 'OK,' he agreed.

'Let's take you up and show you your room,' Connie suggested. She held out a hand, and after a second's hesitation he slipped his into it and stood up. She curled her fingers round the back of his small, soft hand and squeezed comfortingly. 'Bathroom first. Teeth and loo.'

She did his teeth, gave him a little privacy and then ushered him down the corridor. 'Here we are. It used to belong to my brother, but he had an accident and died a long time ago. I expect it will enjoy having another boy staying in it.'

She pushed the door open, and got her first flicker of reaction from him. His eyes tracked to the disreputable old teddy on the pillow, and stayed there. She picked him up, turned down the quilt and sat further down the bed, patting the sheet. 'In you hop.'

He climbed in, slid down so his head was on the pillow and he was flat on his back, and stared at her with empty eyes.

'Shall I tell you a story about Edward?'

'I'm Edward.'

She smiled. 'I know—but so's this bear. He's Teddy Edward, and a long time ago, when Anthony was about your age, they had an adventure. Would you like to hear about it?'

He hesitated, so long that she thought she'd lost him, and then he nodded. 'Yes, please.'

'Right. Well, you see, they'd gone out for a picnic. They had a little bar of chocolate, a fairy cake, a bottle of squash and a jamjar.'

She waited a moment and sure enough, his curiosity overcame him. 'A jamjar?' he asked softly.

She nodded. 'Yes—they were going down to the river to catch minnows before their picnic. Anyway, they settled down on the river bank, Anthony on one side, Teddy Edward on the other, and the picnic in between. Then suddenly, a gust of wind came and blew Teddy Edward into the water!'

Edward's eyes widened. Encouraged, Connie went on. 'Well, Anthony was terribly upset. He came running home, crying his eyes out because he'd lost his best friend in the world, and told my parents what had happened.'

'Did they find him?'

She nodded. 'My father ran back with him to the river and walked along the bank, calling out and searching, until finally, by a humungous miracle, they spotted him. He was stuck in a branch that hung low down over the river, and my father waded in and pulled him out to safety. That's why his fur's all matted and fuzzy, and why he's such a muddy colour, but Anthony still loved him just the same.'

Edward gave a little sigh. 'I haven't got a teddy,' he confessed, his eyes still fixed longingly on Teddy Edward.

'Haven't you?' said Connie, who'd already established that there wasn't such a thing as a teddy bear in Edward's suitcase. 'Well, that's the most extraordinary thing, because Teddy Edward hasn't got a little boy any more, and he's been ever so lonely since my brother died. I don't suppose you'd consider letting him sleep with you, would you? It would make him very happy.'

Edward nodded solemnly, and lifted up the edge of the quilt. Connie tucked the teddy in beside him, kissed them both goodnight and turned down the light.

'I'll be just downstairs, in the sitting room,' she told him. 'Just call if you need anything, all right? And I'll send your Daddy up to see you just the minute he gets in.'

The little head nodded again, and Connie blew him another kiss and went quietly downstairs. She had meant to go straight into the sitting room, but instead she went into the cloakroom, shut herself in, turned on the taps full and howled her eyes out.

Then she washed her face, sniffed hard and raided

her father's bottle of malt whisky while she settled down to wait for Patrick.

'You're still up.'

'Yes. I was waiting up for you.'

One dark brow arched quizzically, but Connie couldn't be bothered with little games.

'Edward's here,' she said economically.

He froze, searching her face, then looked away, then looked back. 'Edward?' he croaked.

'Your son—I believe he's your son?'

He sat down as if someone had cut his strings. 'Yes—but—um—how—?'

'Your wife—I assume your wife?' She paused for confirmation.

'Ex-wife. Very, very definitely ex-wife.'

'Good. Your ex-wife brought him and dropped him off. I rather got the feeling that if I hadn't been here, she would have left him on the step like a bag of jumble.'

Patrick's mouth tightened. 'What did she say?' he asked.

'You want me to repeat it? I'm not sure I can bring myself to say the things she said.'

'In front of him?'

Connie gave a sad little laugh. 'Oh, yes. And to him. I gather that it's not a good idea to allow myself to get pregnant because you're funny about abortion. And Ron doesn't seem to get on too well with him. Oh, and her nanny's chucked it in—'

'I wonder why?' he said drily.

'And she's gone to Antigua for six weeks and will send all his stuff on when she gets back. She said she hopes you'll be very happy together and she only went for custody to annoy you, but it's got boring.'

He stared at her for an age, then he dropped his face into his hands and propped his elbows on his knees. He stayed like that for some time, occasionally shaking his head as if in disbelief, and then he looked up at Connie again, his eyes deep pools of pain and fury.

'Where is he?' he asked softly.

'In my brother's room.'

He hesitated for a moment. 'Won't your parents mind?'

She shook her head. 'Not if they'd seen him, with those great big eyes. And, anyway, it's not a shrine.'

He nodded, and then ran upstairs three at a time. He was gone for half an hour, and when he came down his eyes were filled with tears. She slopped some of her father's ten-year-old single malt into a glass and stuck it in his hand.

'Drink this,' she ordered, and he gulped it, coughed, then took a more cautious sip.

Finally he looked at her. 'Whose is the teddy?'

'My brother's.'

'It's wet,' he told her. 'So's the pillow.'

His voice caught, and he turned round, pacing across the room, glaring at the ceiling until he'd recovered his composure. 'I'll kill her. This time she's gone too far.'

'I got the impression it was what you wanted.'

'Oh, it is, but not like this—like a bag of jumble dropped off outside a village hall.' He slammed the glass down, slopping the contents onto his hand. 'Damn her!' he muttered. 'She really is an evil bitch.'

'So why did you marry her?' Connie said, finally

asking the question that had been plaguing her for hours.

'Because she was pregnant,' he said bitterly, 'and she threatened to have an abortion if I didn't. She fancied being a city doctor's wife, but she rather had in mind some smart little practice on Harley Street, I think, not the wrong end of Putney. It didn't agree with her at all.'

Having met her, Connie could understand that. 'So, what will you do now?'

He shrugged. 'I don't know. I was trying to find a practice somewhere in the country where I could get a nanny-cum-housekeeper to look after him, and bring him up doing the things little boys ought to do, like playing in the village football team and joining the scouts and going fishing—not being left to his own devices in a smart little flat with not so much as a pot plant!'

He sighed heavily and stabbed his hands through his hair. 'I just needed a little more time. I went to look at somewhere last weekend, but I didn't like the practice set-up and it was too expensive, anyway. I asked her to give me another six months, just to get sorted out with the right place, but, oh, no, she'd got to do it her way. Being civilised is nothing like dramatic enough to appeal to her sense of theatre.'

He reached for the whisky and took another swig, then swallowed it carefully. He eyed the glass, then shot a grin at Connie. 'I never drink, you know. I can't remember the last time I had a drink.'

'I just thought you needed it. I thought I did, too.'

'Yes, I'm sorry about involving you in this. Damn, what a mess.' He sighed. 'How was he? Did he seem upset?'

She shook her head. 'He was very, very quiet. Withdrawn. Scared to death, I would say. Perfectly polite, but quite, quite remote.'

Patrick swallowed hard. 'Poor little chap. He's often like that for the first few minutes with me, then he starts to thaw. He's a lovely kid.'

'He is—and I think bringing him up here to you was the best thing she could possibly have done. Having met her, I think that even one more day with her would have been a day too long.'

'And that's your conservative opinion?'

She blushed. 'Sorry. I always did run off at the mouth about things that affect me.'

'And he affected you?'

'You should have seen him, Patrick. He looked so small there on the drive…' Her voice fizzled out, and she sniffed and took a gulp of her whisky. It burned all the way down and made her cough, but at least she could feel it. She got the feeling the mother could drink neat acid without noticing.

'Does she have a name, by the way?'

'To help you find a focus for your hatred?'

Connie's eyes locked with Patrick's for a long moment, and she sighed. 'I'm sorry. It's none of my business.'

'Yes, it is. She made it your business when she left Edward in your care. Her name's Marina.'

Connie nodded. How appropriate for such a cold fish. 'I don't actually hate her,' she mused out loud. 'I feel intensely sorry for her, and I'm angry with her, but I don't hate her. She can't be normal, giving up her child like that to pursue some fleeting happiness.'

Patrick smiled slightly. 'Thank you for that. I do try not to hate her. I don't know that I've ever loved her, and she lied to me about being on the Pill. I think she was just going to slip off to a clinic if the worst came to the worst, but the trouble was, as a doctor, I was too fast to catch on to her symptoms. And that left marriage.'

'Old-fashioned, isn't it?'

'I wanted to protect the child. Tell me I was wrong to do that, Connie.'

She shook her head. 'I can't. Of course you were right. It's just that most people wouldn't have bothered.'

'Well, I'm not most people, and I'm going to have a crisis on my hands in the morning as a result, because I've got surgery to get through and Edward to keep me company. I suppose he can sit in the office with the ladies, but that gives me a day and a half to find a nanny before Monday morning.'

Connie didn't have a choice. Her mouth took over, speaking for her heart without bothering to consult her head. 'I'll look after him, if you like. I'm stuck here until my arm heals, and I'm bored to death.'

He searched her face, hope in his eyes, then the hope faded. 'But you hate kids. You said today if you had a child you'd send it to boarding school at the age of one.'

'Patrick, I was joking,' she laughed.

He didn't smile. 'I daren't risk it, Connie. He's had a mother who found him too much trouble. There's no way he's having a nanny who feels the same way, even if it is just for a short while.'

'He's no trouble!' she protested. 'Patrick, I was joking earlier. I love children! For God's sake, I'm a paediatrician—'

'A neonatal paediatric surgeon. That's not quite the same thing as a nanny.'

She sighed. 'No, it isn't, but the feeling for the children is essentially the same. Health, happiness, well-being, security. Patrick, I'm here. We got on well, I think. At least let me help you until you find someone who's right to do the job.'

He hesitated, then stood up. 'Can I think about it? I have to be sure, Connie. You must see that. I'd like to watch you in action together before I decide. And, anyway, I think you need time to consider, too. I don't want you taking him on as a knee-jerk reaction and then regretting it or finding it too much.'

He had a point. She always had been impulsive. 'All right. That seems fair. We'll talk about it again tomorrow.'

'Thanks—and thank you for all you've done tonight—well, all day, in fact. I'm very grateful, for all of it, but especially for looking after Edward. And thanks for giving him the teddy, that was really thoughtful.'

She smiled, a sad little smile. 'It's nice to see him being loved again. Anthony even took him to university. It seemed such an obvious thing to do, to give him to Edward.'

'Not to everyone,' Patrick said flatly, and Connie knew he was talking about Marina and the fact that she would never have given such a disreputable old toy house room.

'No, perhaps not to everyone,' she agreed. She stood up, suddenly dreadfully weary. 'Goodnight, Patrick. I'll see you in the morning.'

And she went upstairs, checked her little charge and went to bed.

Patrick didn't know which way to turn. Connie seemed such an obvious answer, but she had found the children at the clinic a trial—or at least, she'd said so. She'd said she was joking, but what if there was an element of truth? What if she really did find it all too much?

He sighed and switched on the beside light. He couldn't sleep, not with his son arriving unannounced in the icy blast of Marina's dismissal, and Connie so cross with her for hurting the little one, and his own feelings for Edward so raw and full of guilt.

There was a little cry, and before he knew he was doing it, he leapt out of bed and ran to his son. Curiously, he met Connie on the landing, similarly hurrying, and they exchanged a rueful laugh.

'I'll deal with him. You've done more than enough, Connie, thanks.'

She hovered, then nodded and went back to her room. He went in, turning up the light a fraction, and found Edward still asleep, mumbling and tossing and turning restlessly. 'It's all right, sprog, Daddy's here,' he murmured, and Edward's eyes flickered open.

'Daddy?' he said.

'I'm here, love. Can't you sleep well?'

'I had a dream,' he said.

'I know.' Patrick couldn't leave him alone, and there was no room for him in the narrow single bed. 'I tell you what—do you want to come and cuddle up with me, just for tonight? It's all a bit strange, isn't it?'

'Will it be all right?' he asked anxiously.

'Of course it will be all right.'

'What about Connie? Won't she mind?'

For a moment Patrick didn't understand, but then

suddenly the penny dropped and he had to clamp down on his anger. 'Connie's just a friend,' he explained. 'I'm looking after her daddy's patients while he's sick. She's not my girlfriend, sproglet. Just a chum.'

The child took a moment to absorb that, then nodded. 'OK. Can Teddy Edward come, too?'

Patrick picked the old bear up and put him on his son's chest. 'Of course.' He scooped the boy up into his arms and carried him across the landing to his own room, putting him down on the big double bed. In minutes they were both asleep, Patrick flat on his back spreadeagled across the bed, Edward snuggled up close with one heavy, possessive arm around his shoulders and the bear under his chin.

That was how Connie found them in the morning.

'Won't it make a dreadful mess?' Edward asked anxiously.

Connie looked up from the bowl of chopped-up chocolate caramel bars and surveyed the worried little face. 'Very probably,' she agreed. 'That's why we're wearing old clothes and aprons. Besides,' she added, 'it makes it more fun if it's messy. Right, you have to help me. I'll stir this over the hot water, because I can do that with one hand, but I want you to open the packet of crispies for me with the scissors. Can you do that?'

She gave him the blunt-ended kitchen scissors, held the wrapper up so he could see and had to prevent herself from hugging him because he looked so delicious when he was concentrating. His little tongue came out and sat in the corner of his mouth, and his ears went pink with concentration.

Finally, the top was cut open, and he put the scissors down. 'Is that all right?'

'Excellent. Right, I'll stir this, and you can pour them in, a little at a time. Can you manage?'

The short answer was, not really, but she didn't care. He overshot the bowl and the dogs ended up with a delicious treat. Edward, however, froze until she looked down at the hopeful dogs and sighed.

'Do you want more?'

They wagged their tails, and she told them to wait. 'Right, Edward, pour a little into each of their bowls, please, and then perhaps we'll get some peace. That's right. Now, tell them they can have it. Say good cats.'

'But they're not cats!' he said with what was almost a giggle.

'So what are they?'

'Good dogs!' he said, and the dogs dived into the bowls head first.

And then, finally, he did laugh, a tiny chuckle suppressed almost before it was out, but nevertheless it was progress.

Thank God for that, Connie thought, and then drew his attention back to the chocolate crispy bars they were supposed to be making. 'Come on, then, let's have a few more for us. Tip them in.'

He was better at it the second time, and she stirred with her left hand as he poured, his tongue jammed in the corner of his mouth, his ears positively glowing.

'There, that's enough,' she said, and stirred until the crispies were evenly coated.

'Now, this is the bit I need you to do because I really can't manage it with only one hand. If I tip the bowl up, will you scrape it all out into this dish and then squash it down flat? Then we'll put it in the fridge to get chilly, and we can have some for lunch with Daddy!'

He had been right. It was hideously messy, but she didn't care. They had enormous fun, and she made sure there was lots of licking out of the bowl to be done at the end.

He would probably be sick, she thought, wedging the pan in the fridge, but there you go.

'Right, while that gets chilled we need to do some clearing up, OK? If you wipe the floor, I'll wipe the table. Sound fair?'

He nodded, and she gave him a cloth and watched as he squirmed around under the table, blotting up crispies that the dogs had missed. She wiped the table, washed out the cloth and squeezed it out with her left hand, then looked round to see how Edward was doing.

He was scrubbing at a spot on his knee with the cloth, a worried frown on his face, and she took the cloth from him and smiled. 'All done now.'

'My trousers,' he said in a stage whisper.

'Look like ordinary trousers to me,' she said. 'They'll wash.'

'Mummy gets cross if I get dirty.'

Connie struggled for diplomacy. 'Well, we're in the country now,' she explained, 'and with all the dogs and cows and fishing and stuff, it's hard to keep clean for long so we don't tend to worry so much as they might in town.'

'So it's all right to get dirty?'

She nodded. 'Yes, of course—especially if they aren't your best clothes. Even in the country we try to keep *them* clean.'

He seemed to relax then, and Connie heaved an inward sigh of relief and put the cloth in the sink. 'I tell you what, why don't we take the dogs for a little walk up to the shop, buy the paper and come back? By then the crispy bars should be ready to eat.'

So they did, not worrying about coats because it was such a lovely warm September day. She let Edward take Toby because he was such a softy, and she took Rolo who was younger and more inclined to rush after cats, and they wandered up the village street and back.

The dogs thought it was a bit of a sorry walk, but she didn't want to overtire Edward, and she hadn't told anyone she was going out. As it was they were gone nearly half an hour, and when they arrived back Patrick was pacing in the kitchen.

'Hello, sproglet,' he said with artificial calm. 'Been for a walk?'

'We took the dogs and bought the paper—and, look, we made crispy cake bars!' He pulled the fridge door open and the pan of crispy cake slid out and headed for the floor.

Connie fielded it in the nick of time, but Edward looked horrified. Connie just laughed. 'Good job I caught it or we would have had squashy cakes instead,' she joked.

The tension eased, and suddenly, to her relief and amazement, he started to giggle. 'Squashy cakes,' he said, and doubled up, laughing.

Connie's eyes filled with tears and she turned away, but not before Patrick had seen her. He made tea, and they sat down round the table with tea or squash and not-quite-chilled crispy bars, and Edward chattered happily about what they'd been doing that morning.

Then he ran to the cloakroom, and Patrick caught her eye.

'Thank you,' he said fervently. 'There have been times when I thought he'd never laugh again.'

She swallowed. 'Anytime. Jokes we do for free.'

'Connie, did you mean it last night when you offered to look after him?'

She opened her mouth to say she was still thinking about it, but her heart got there first again. 'Of course,' she said, and discovered she meant it.

'Good. Because, if you could bear to do it, I'd like you to look after him, at least for the immediate future. I need to find somewhere to live, and goodness knows where that will be, but it's pointless trying to find anyone permanent until we have more idea.'

She nodded. 'OK. I'll do whatever you want. As you know, I'm sitting here twiddling my thumbs—or, at least, my thumb. The right one doesn't seem to want to twiddle to order.'

'How about that sling?' Patrick suggested. 'You really ought to rest it more.'

'While I'm housekeeping? I hardly think so.'

'It's only cooking. We can have instant meals. I'll pay you, even just to nuke them in the microwave, if it means I don't have to worry about Edward. And all your food's thrown in, of course.'

'Fine. Sounds like a good deal. I like the thought of being paid just to fire up the microwave.'

'And make chocolate crispy cakes.'

'And make chocolate crispy cakes.'

'And wear your sling.'

Connie grinned. 'OK. And wear my sling. It's a deal.'

CHAPTER FIVE

CONNIE tried to wear her sling. She really did try, but it got in the way and she found it difficult to do things with Edward—like dress him, and bath him, and hug him.

At first he wouldn't let her hug him, but after a few days he would snuggle up to her side to look at a book, and if her arm crept round him, he'd allow it.

And that, for Connie, was so precious that she wasn't letting some old sling get in the way.

Her father was progressing well, but her parents had decided that, rather than come home, they'd go to a special convalescent hotel on the south coast for a couple of weeks when the time came. She took Edward to Cambridge to meet them, and told them that he was staying in Anthony's room, and to her relief they seemed genuinely pleased.

He had Teddy Edward with him, and her mother's eyes filled a little when she saw the ragged little bear.

'Do you mind?' Connie asked her softly, and she shook her head and smiled and blinked the tears away.

'No, of course not. It just brings back a lot of lovely memories.'

Connie nodded. She could understand that perfectly. She'd found the same thing, spending so much time in Anthony's room. It had brought back much of her childhood, and the memories were bitter sweet.

Anthony would have adored Edward, Connie knew.

He'd had a girlfriend with a little boy at the time he was killed, and he'd been wonderful with him.

'How's Patrick getting on? Still coping all right?' her father asked with a thread of concern.

'He's fine. He's doing a great job. The receptionists all love him, and the patients think he's marvellous— you'll have your work cut out when you come home,' she teased, and intercepted a glance between her parents.

'What?'

'Nothing, darling. We're just wondering how long it will be before your father feels up to it. He'll probably go back part time at first, and get another locum to fill in. I don't suppose Patrick will want half time.'

So he'll leave, Connie thought, and take Edward. She glanced down at the little tow-coloured head bent earnestly over a puzzle on the floor, and felt a huge pang of loss.

No. That was silly. Of course Patrick was going— she'd always known that. He was looking at a place at the moment, up in Yorkshire, and wouldn't be back until late that night.

Yorkshire was so far…

'Still, I expect it will be a couple of months, at least, before I'm well enough to do even that much,' her father was saying, 'so I hope Patrick's happy to stay until then. I'd hate to lose him.'

'I'm sure that will be all right,' she said, crossing her fingers surreptitiously under the edge of the bedclothes.

'Now, young lady, how about your arm?' her father asked.

'It's fine,' Connie lied.

'Let me see.'

'Daddy, stop fussing. You're off duty.'

'You're my daughter. Let me see it. Thank you. Right, now wiggle your fingers.'

She tried to wiggle, but they were slow and unresponsive and vague.

'Hmm. Grip my finger.'

She tried. She really did try very, very hard to squeeze, but her thumb and the first couple of fingers were very weak still. 'It's taking a long time to recover,' she told him. 'It still hurts a bit. I expect if they take the plates out in a few months it will improve.'

Tom Wright met his daughter's eyes and smiled gently. 'I expect so,' he said, with that comforting note that meant he was lying.

Oh, God. She couldn't even bear to think about what might happen to her if it didn't recover. If she couldn't go back to surgery, whatever would she do? Paediatric medicine, of course, which was what she'd started training for, but they didn't like it if you weren't single-minded, and it could mess up your career prospects. Just when she'd been getting on so well, too.

Oh, hell.

Her mother was bent over, helping Edward with the last piece of the puzzle, and when it was in she clapped and cheered. 'Clever boy! Well done. Now, pick all the pieces up and put them back in the toy box, and we'll see if there's anything else you want to play with.'

Connie felt a lump in her throat. Her mother would have been so good with grandchildren, but Anthony was dead and there was no one in Connie's life at the moment even remotely interested in her.

Except Patrick, a little voice said, and she dismissed it because she simply didn't think it was true.

Which was a great shame, because it suddenly registered like a clap of thunder that she'd fallen for Patrick and his adorable little son, and losing them in a few weeks or months or whatever it would be was going to tear her apart...

It was no good. The practice was run down, old-fashioned and it seemed everyone liked it that way. Certainly Patrick with his new ideas and driving energy wasn't what they were looking for, and so he set off on the long road back to Essex with a heavy heart.

The hills gave way to the flat land of the fens, and then the gently rolling fields of Suffolk. He headed south from Ipswich, turned left before Colchester and wound down the now-familiar little lanes to Great Ashley.

This, of course, was his perfect practice, but Tom Wright was hoping to hang on for a few more years and there was no way Patrick could wait that long, especially not with Edward now in his care.

He sighed. He was using Connie, he knew it, but she and the boy seemed so genuinely contented together, and she tried so hard to keep everything low-key and not overface the child.

She encouraged him to get dirty, to puggle about in the mud, to stamp in puddles, to do all the awful things little boys did, and bit by bit, inch by inch, he was starting to flourish.

There was colour in his cheeks, and laughter every now and then, though not as often as Patrick would like, and he was sleeping better now. For the last week he'd been in his own bed, without crossing the landing more than a couple of times for a cuddle and some reassurance.

That had to mean something.

He turned onto the drive, parked the car and went in. It was late, almost ten, and he could hear soft music from the sitting room. He hung up his jacket on the bottom of the banisters, put his head round the door— and smiled.

Connie was curled up on the sofa, lashes down against her peach-soft skin, fast asleep. She looked about as old as Edward, and a funny, protective surge ran through him.

He made tea and poked about in the fridge for something to eat. He was starving, and he wondered if she'd left him anything, but he couldn't see an obvious plate or whatever.

'Hi.'

He straightened and turned, just as she smiled and lifted up her hair, tunnelling her fingers through it and tossing it back off her shoulders with a little shake of the head. She looked warm and sleepy and unbelievably desirable, and he forgot about being tired and hungry. Well, that sort of hungry, anyway.

The other sort—that was more difficult to forget, with Connie padding softly round the kitchen in her little bare feet with those astonishingly erotic toes tipped with siren red, and that damned perfume of hers curling round his insides and turning them to fire. As young as Edward? Not by light years!

'Are you hungry? I thought you might have eaten on the way, but there's some bacon in the fridge if you want a sandwich.'

She tipped her head up, just a foot or so away from him, and his breath stopped in his throat. He wanted to kiss her. He wanted it so badly he thought he'd choke on it so he went over to the kettle and busied himself at the sink.

'That would be lovely,' he murmured gruffly. 'Have you eaten?'

'I had something with Edward, but that was hours ago. I could manage a bacon sandwich, I'm sure.'

She bustled about, struggling with one hand, and he forced himself to leave her to it and made a pot of tea.

'How did you get on?' she asked as she worked. 'Any good?'

'No. They're pre-NHS, almost. It was hopeless. I'd fit in like a naked female mud-wrestler in a monastery.'

'That good, eh?' she said with a chuckle, and drifted past him to get plates. Her perfume curled round him again, and he gritted his teeth and shoved his hands into his pockets to keep them from grabbing her.

'So, what have you two done today?' he asked, pouring the tea and sitting down out of the way once she'd gone back to the stove.

'Oh, we went to see my parents. They thought Edward was lovely, and they're quite happy about the room, which I knew they would be, and Dad wondered if you'd be able to stay on another couple of months until he's well enough to come back part time.'

'And what then?'

She shrugged. 'I think he thought you'd want to move on to something more permanent by then so he was talking about a part-time locum, perhaps half-time.'

Patrick nodded thoughtfully, his mind whirling. Two months to find a place and settle Edward with a new nanny, and break into a new community, and start all over again.

Just in time for the new millennium, he thought. A fresh start for us both.

The thought was curiously lonely.

'I expect that would be all right,' he said, biting into his sandwich. 'How about you? Are you OK for the next two months?'

There was a slightly haunted look to her eyes, he thought, or was he imagining it? 'Should be fine. My arm's taking its time to heal, so I might as well do this as sit about and do nothing. Edward's a love, anyway, so it's not exactly a hardship.'

He dropped his eyes to her fingers, sticking out of the end of her cast like pale, slender sausages. 'How is the arm? Really?'

She shifted it, tucking it into her lap. 'OK. Pain seems better. I hardly take any of those pills. The sling seems to be helping it.'

'When you remember to wear it. You're a bad girl—that was part of our deal.'

'So sue me,' she said, taking a huge bite of her sandwich and meeting his eyes defiantly.

God, she was lovely! He felt his mouth tip up at the corners but was powerless to prevent it. He wanted to drag her into his arms and kiss her senseless. He had another bite of sandwich instead, and let it all wash over him.

Life was complicated enough without him making it worse.

'Can I tack Mr Ray on the end of your list?' Tanya asked Patrick, popping her head round the door between patients. 'He rang up just now, and he sounds awful. He wanted to see you tonight, but he sounded so bad I told him we were too busy and could he possibly come now. Is that OK?'

Patrick nodded. 'Thanks. That's fine. What sort of awful? Does he need a visit?'

She laughed. 'Probably. He's got a dreadful cough and he sounds very breathless, but he wouldn't call you out unless it was to write his death certificate.'

Patrick smiled. 'Another one of those tough old boys. Yeah, sure, tack him on. Good idea.'

He saw the next two patients, and then heard Mr Ray arrive through the closed door. His cough was harsh and continuous, and Patrick was immediately concerned. He led him through to the consulting room, sat him in the chair and listened to his chest, then sat back and tutted.

'Mr Ray, how long have you been like this?'

'What, this bit of a cough?' he asked, breaking off to cough again. 'Couple of days—maybe more. Thought it was getting a bit troublesome—must have caught a chill that wet day we had last week.'

Patrick sighed and shook his head imperceptibly. 'Mr Ray, you've got more than a bit of a cough. I'm afraid you've got pneumonia. You're going to have to go to hospital.'

'Hospital? Never been to hospital in my life. Been fit as a flea.'

'I'm sure, but you aren't now. I'm sorry, I really can't let you stay at home. You need some serious antibiotics and oxygen to help you get better.'

'Oh. Well. I suppose if I have to, I have to. What about my animals?'

'Are you a stock farmer?'

'No—just a few chickens and the dog and cats. I

suppose my neighbours could do it—they're good people. They'd go in and feed them, if I asked. Got the dog in the car, as a matter of fact.'

'You drove here?' Patrick asked, horrified.

'How d'you think I got here, then? Walked? It's five miles, boy!'

Patrick thought for a moment, then had an idea. 'What's the dog like? Civilised? House-trained?'

'It's a lovely dog. Sleeps with me, matter of fact.'

'Spoilt to death, then,' Patrick said with a grin. 'I was wondering if he'd be all right with Dr Wright's two dogs.'

'Should be. He's used to other dogs. What did you have in mind?'

Patrick shrugged. 'Well, he could always stay here until lunchtime and we could run him back later and talk to your neighbour. You'd only be in hospital for a few days, a week at the most. We could make sure your neighbour was happy about it, and give him a key, to save you going back there.'

'Sounds grand. His name's Killer. He's in the back of the pickup—' Another fit of coughing had Patrick reaching for the phone. He rang the hospital, arranged for Mr Ray's admission and then went and broke the glad tidings to Connie.

'But I can't drive with the cast on!' she protested.

'Nonsense. You can drive my car, it's an automatic. I'm sure you can manage it with one and a half hands. I'll drive the pickup.'

'But what if the dog's awful? What if Toby and Rolo want to kill it?'

Patrick looked down in amazement at the two dogs lying each side of Connie's feet like bookends. 'Is that a serious suggestion?' he said comically.

Connie's eyes followed his, and she shrugged. 'So they look quiet and peaceful. Even tigers have to sleep.'

Patrick snorted, convinced she was worrying about nothing, and he was fortunately right. As it turned out, Killer was nothing of the sort.

He was a great, hairy lurcher, a leggy, straggly hound of indeterminate origin with enough of some sort of gazehound in him to justify the term 'lurcher', but not enough to give him any intrinsic grace or good looks. He settled down on the floor by the door, whined occasionally and gave off the general odour of fox mess from a nice patch of crispy hair behind one ear.

Connie thought he was actually rather sweet if he didn't smell so bad, but she kept Edward away from him just to be on the safe side. Toby and Rolo sniffed around him for a while, but then lay down, one eye apiece just cracked open, checking him out while they dozed.

She and Edward were doing puzzles at the kitchen table, fitting together interlocking shapes to build a simple three-D tower. It was fairly easy, but too much for him on his own, and it was the only toy in his suitcase. Connie vowed to send Patrick toy-shopping one day soon.

They had just put the last piece in when Patrick came through from the surgery. 'Right. Would you two like to jump in the car, and I'll take Killer in the pickup— Good grief, whatever is that *awful* smell?'

Edward seemed to shrink, but Connie laughed. 'Fox mess, I think. My mother calls it "the great smell of woof". These two have been known to partake of it on occasions.'

Patrick looked at the dog in disbelief. 'Well, it's certainly not Chanel,' he said drily. 'Right, come on, then. I suggest you follow me, so we don't lose each other.'

He handed her the keys, called Killer and went out of the kitchen door into the car park. Connie followed, telling the dogs to stay, and then had the problem of putting the keys in the ignition on the right hand side of the steering column with her left hand.

Not easy. Fortunately the car started with the first turn of the key and, being an automatic, she simply had to aim it. Well, she thought, at least I know I can drive an automatic if the worst comes to the worst, and then felt vaguely sick.

Was it really a possibility? She thought she'd felt a little more sensation the past few days, but had she been deluding herself?

What if it never came back? What if her hand remained nerveless and feeble? She wouldn't even be able to give injections properly, or set up drips, or do any of the other many things a physician had to do. It wasn't only surgeons who needed two hands. What if she couldn't go back to medicine at all?

'Connie? What's the matter?'

She turned round and looked at Edward, strapped onto his booster cushion in the back seat. 'Nothing, darling. I'm just concentrating. I've never driven Patrick's car before.'

She tried to keep her mind on the job, watching Killer in the back of the pickup and making sure she didn't lose them.

She didn't, and she was happy to hand over to Patrick and slide into the other seat. He found the neighbour, gave him the key and then turned to Edward and Connie. 'Fancy a pub lunch?' he asked.

'Have you got time?'

'Should have. Sound good?'

They both nodded. 'Anywhere special?' Connie asked.

'There's a thatched place we passed.'

'The Three Horseshoes. It's good.'

'So I'd heard. Let's give it a whirl.'

Connie and Patrick had baguettes stuffed with prawns and salad, and Edward had cheese and pickle sandwiches and pinched some of Connie's prawns. It was difficult to eat with one and a half hands, and one of the prawns fell down inside the cast.

'Oh, yuck!' she squeaked, and tried to shake it out, but it wouldn't come. Patrick tried to poke it out, and Edward had to see, but in the end she had to wait until they were back at the surgery before Patrick could extract it with a pair of forceps.

'There. Want to eat it?' he teased, offering it to her in the jaws of the forceps, but she pushed it away, laughing a little humourlessly.

'Patrick, don't,' she said, and he lowered the forceps slowly and looked at her.

'Connie? What is it?'

'I need this cast off,' she told him a little petulantly. 'My arm's healed and it's just a nuisance now. I can't be bothered to go back to London. Could you do it?'

'You need a plaster saw—and anyway, you ought to go back and see your consultant.'

'No!' she exclaimed, and then shook her head. 'I don't want to see her.'

'Because she's going to tell you what you don't want to hear?'

Connie turned away, hanging onto her control by a thread. 'No, she's not. She's just going to tell me off for not resting it. I'll go next week.'

And she escaped back into the house to Edward, who didn't ask difficult questions and who kept her busy enough that she didn't have to think about it.

Patrick was getting worried about Connie. He was sure she'd missed at least one follow-up appointment, and he decided to tackle her again about it later.

For now, though, he was too busy. The practice nurse, Jane Pierce, was running a routine surgery that afternoon, and he had a couple of hours off, technically speaking, in which to catch up with his admin, write a few hundred referral letters and get straight.

It was not to be. Jane popped her head round the door with an apologetic smile. 'I don't suppose you could come and have a look at this, could you? It's Mrs Brown. She's had a leg ulcer under treatment for months, and it's just stubbornly refused to heal, and I think I can see something in the bottom of it.'

'Something?' he said, getting up and following her across to her room. 'What sort of something? Hello, Mrs Brown, I gather you've got an ulcer that doesn't seem to want to get better.'

'That's right,' she said. 'You take a look. Sister Pierce reckons she can see something in it, though I can't imagine what, unless a little splinter of metal broke off the supermarket trolley, but it didn't bleed— just hurt like the dickens.'

Patrick bent over and shone a little torch onto the ulcer, and there was a distinct metallic gleam at the base.

'Seems so silly,' Mrs Brown went on. 'It was only

a little knock with a trolley, and it's been going on for months now, and I didn't have anything like this much trouble when I broke the blessed thing.'

Patrick straightened up slowly. 'You broke it?'

'Yes, five years ago. Had it pinned and plated.'

Patrick chuckled. 'I think that's your answer, then. I think the trolley's hit the skin over one of the screws. Maybe you ought to go back to the consultant and have the screws out—is there a record in the notes?'

Jane nodded. 'Yes—here it is. I didn't notice it— how silly of me.'

'Well, it was a long time ago, dear. I forgot about it myself,' Mrs Brown said kindly. 'So, will he be able to take them out?'

'I'm sure he will. I'll give him a ring. Stay here, and I'll do it from this phone. I might need to ask you questions.'

The consultant was busy, but his secretary took a note of all the details and agreed it would need seeing to as a matter of urgency. 'I'll get him to contact Mrs Brown direct and make an appointment,' she said.

'Oh, well,' said Mrs Brown when he relayed that, 'at least my husband won't be able to say I've gone screwy any more, will he?'

She was still wheezing and chuckling when Patrick went back to his room. He shook his head, amazed at her cheerfulness and how well she'd taken it. If only Connie could be so brave and philosophical, but he guessed she had more at stake than Mrs Brown.

Still, she had to go and face the music some time. He caught up with her later in the sitting room, after Edward was in bed.

'Connie, about seeing your consultant—' he began, but she wasn't having any of it.

'Patrick, mind your own business,' she said harshly. 'It's nothing to do with you, savvy? It's *my* arm—'

'Connie, for heaven's sake, I'm only trying to help! It needs following up! Quite obviously it's not healing without residual damage, and if you need nothing else you need a programme of intensive physio to minimise the long-term effects of that damage—'

'There is no permanent damage! Why can't you get that into your head? It's getting better, Patrick! It is— it's just taking time.'

He shook his head. 'No, Connie, it's not just time. It's worse than that, and you know it.'

She swallowed convulsively, and he felt a real heel, but she had to face it, had to go and see her specialist and deal with it. 'Connie, you do know it, and that's the trouble, isn't it?'

'I don't know it, and you don't know it either. You're just jumping to conclusions and telling me what to do. Well, let me tell you something,' she said, poking him in the chest with her left index finger, 'you're not my doctor, and you can't tell me what to do. You can tell me how to do my job with Edward, fine, but when it comes to my health and my arm, that's *my* business, and it's nothing to do with you, and I don't want to hear what you think!'

And with that she ran out, slamming the door behind her. He heard her footsteps drumming up the stairs, then her bedroom door shut with a defiant crash.

Patrick followed her with a sigh. All the slamming was bound to have woken up Edward, and no doubt he was going to have to deal with it. He went into the boy's room and found him lying there wide-eyed.

'Is Connie cross with me?' he asked in a strangled whisper.

He sat down on the edge of the bed and patted Edward's hand. 'No, little sprog, she's cross with me. I tried to tell her what to do, and she didn't like it.'

'Oh. Will she go away?'

He sighed and hugged the little boy. 'No, I don't think so. Even if she does, I won't. I'm afraid you're stuck with me for ever, whatever happens about the other people in our lives. Can you bear it?'

Edward's little arms tightened around his neck, but he didn't say a word. Patrick hugged him tighter, choked by the child's fearful eyes and hideous insecurity. Damn Marina for doing this to him, he thought, and that was followed by a wave of guilt for leaving him with her and assuming that just because she was his mother, he'd be all right.

How wrong he'd been!

And he was wrong to have bullied Connie. He hadn't seen the X-rays, he didn't know the exact extent of the damage, and he couldn't tell how much or how little progress she was making.

Only she knew all of that, and she was right—it was her business, not his.

Oh, hell.

'I tell you what, little guy, in the morning we'll make Connie breakfast in bed and take it in there to say I'm sorry for upsetting her, OK? Will you help me do that?'

Edward's little head nodded against his shoulder. 'OK,' he whispered.

Connie was woken by a tap on the door. She'd had a restless, unhappy night, plagued by guilt and tormented by the fear of what she was going to have to do, and the last thing she wanted was to face anyone.

Then she heard Edward's little voice.

She sat up, shoved her pillows up the bed and told him to come in. He came, bearing a plate of toast and marmalade in wobbly hands, tongue wedged in the corner of his mouth, eyes fixed on the toast that was just beginning to slide perilously close to the edge of the plate.

She leaned over and corrected the slope in the nick of time, and smiled at him. 'Is that for me?' she asked, less than enthused. What she really wanted was a cup of tea, but she wasn't going to tell him that!

'Yes—and Daddy says, have you forgiven him, an' he's got a tea tray if you have.'

Her heart melted. 'Of course I've forgiven him. Actually, I'd like to see him. Is he there?'

'He is,' said a gruff voice, sleep-roughened and sexy and very, very dear. She felt a huge lump in her throat and swallowed it.

'Come in, Patrick.'

He came in, set the tray down and looked at her with a rueful grin. 'I'm sorry, Connie. I was way out of line. Forgive me?'

She smiled back and reached out a hand, drawing him down onto the edge of the bed. 'Of course I do. Actually, I was going to tell you that you're right, of course. I do need to go. Could you find someone else to have Edward one day next week, if I can get an appointment?'

'Of course—except that I don't really know where to start in the village. Do you think you could find someone?'

She nodded. 'There's a child-minder. She's lovely—she was at school with me, and she's really nice. Edward, if I can get hold of Penny, would you mind going to her for the day and doing some painting and things while I go to London? I have to see my doctor about my arm, and I can't really take you with me all that way. It would be awfully boring for you.'

Edward looked thoughtful. 'Is she nice?' he asked. When Connie said, yes, she was very nice, he added, 'You are coming back, aren't you?'

Connie's eyes filled. 'Oh, sweetheart, of course I'm coming back. It's just for the day. Did you think I wouldn't?'

He shrugged his little shoulders in a gesture far too old for him. 'Maybe.'

She used her good arm to help him up onto the bed, tucked him in beside her and passed him a piece of toast. 'I'm coming back. OK?'

'OK.'

'Right, that's that settled. Patrick, I would do almost anything for a cup of tea,' she said with a smile, and he handed her a steaming mug.

'Here. Mind, it's—'

'Hot,' she finished for him. 'Thank you, Mummy.'

'He's Daddy,' Edward said, confused, and she laughed.

'He's just mothering me,' she explained, and then wondered if Edward actually knew what mothering was, and what it was supposed to be like, and she could have cried for him.

CHAPTER SIX

'So, how is it?'

The consultant waited expectantly for Connie to fill her in, and for the first time she had to tell the absolute truth.

'It—hurts,' she said. 'The median nerve particularly seems to be affected. I'm getting tingling and pins and needles and aching at night, especially, and because the radial nerve is a little bit the same I've been trying to kid myself the cast is tight and pressing on the carpal tunnel, but I know it's junk.'

The consultant nodded. 'OK. Well, the X-rays show a good degree of union, which is very satisfactory after only nine weeks, so I think we'll have the cast off and then I'll have a look and see how it really is.'

Connie nodded, and went out to the plaster room. She was dreading having the cast off, in a way, because the truth would be out then, and she wouldn't be able to lie to herself any longer.

She gritted her teeth and watched as the saw whizzed up the cast and the nurse cracked the two halves away, and then could have wept at the shrivelled, scaly, skinny little limb that was exposed.

'Right, let's give that a little wash and put some hand cream on it, and you'll soon feel better,' the nurse said comfortingly. She was right. The hot water felt wonderful, and for the first time in weeks her hand felt really clean.

The nurse was gentle massaging in the cream, but

it still felt really strange, partly, she supposed, because the nerve supply to the skin was disrupted. It was like going to the dentist and having an injection—you could feel things, vaguely, but it all felt very weird.

'Right, how's that?'

'Lovely. Thank you,' she managed, and looked at it. It didn't seem too odd, strangely. Still a bit thin, of course, but a lot better for the wash and brush up. At least the incisions had healed cleanly.

She went back and waited for the consultant, and after a few agonising minutes she was called in. Her palms were prickling, her mouth felt dry and her heart was pounding. So much hung on it, on whether the consultant felt it could improve or not, given sufficient time.

'Let's have a look then,' the woman said with a smile. 'Right, I want to you stretch it out for me. I know it feels odd, after having your elbow bent for so long, but do the best you can. That's great. Can you rotate your hand? Well done. How did it feel?'

Connie was breaking out in a sweat. 'OK. I feel very nervous.'

'It's all very vulnerable, isn't it? Well, I think orthopaedically it looks good. I think we just need to examine the nerves now. Lay your hand down on here for me, and let's see what you can feel and what you can do.'

The consultant ran through a whole series of pin-pricks, scratches, resisted movements against her fingers, making Connie pull up and push down against her, bending her digits, pinching with thumb and index finger, gripping and so forth.

Then, finally, she sat back and met Connie's eyes. 'Well, I have to say it's not looking good at the moment. We felt that at the time, though, didn't we? The nerve damage was quite extensive, and we were hoping for a significant improvement, but I have to say I was hoping for a better result by now. How do you feel about that?'

Connie looked away, blinking back the tears. 'Well, I think I knew it was coming,' she confessed. 'It's just—will I ever be able to go back to surgery? Is it still too early to tell?'

The consultant tapped a pen thoughtfully for a moment. Connie thought she was probably wondering how hard she could hit her all at once. That was what she would have been doing in her place.

'I would say, on balance, that the likelihood of a complete recovery is now extremely remote. That doesn't mean it won't continue to improve. I think it probably will, and I would like you to have a scan so we can determine if there's any surgical intervention that might improve things, particularly in the median nerve. But, generally speaking, I would say that after this long we would have hoped for more improvement.'

'That's a no, isn't it?' Connie said flatly.

The consultant nodded slowly. 'Yes. I'm afraid it probably is. I think we need the scan results before we can be completely sure, and I want you to see the physio and get a programme of exercises, and then I want to see you again in four weeks. We'll talk about it more then.'

Connie dredged up a smile. 'Thank you. I'll go and see the physio and make an appointment.'

'OK. And Connie? I'm sorry.'

Connie's smile wavered, and she left the room with as much dignity as she could muster. She was *en route* to the physio when a colleague accosted her in the corridor.

'Hey, Connie, you're back!'

She shook her head, still too overcome to chatter. 'Not really. Just had my cast off. It'll be a while yet.'

'But you are coming back?' he persisted.

'Maybe. I'll let you know. I must fly, Doug, I'm late to physio.'

She dived into the physiotherapy department, tried to pay attention to the exercises and then caught a taxi to the station. She was home within two hours, and because Penny had said she was happy to keep Edward until Patrick finished work she was free.

She changed into jeans and an old jumper, pulled on her wellies and a thick coat and walked down to the river with the dogs. It was wet underfoot, but that didn't worry any of them: The dogs didn't care, and Connie hardly noticed.

Her arm ached. Her elbow and wrist felt very weak and vulnerable without the cast, and she tucked her hand into her coat pocket for support.

So that was that, then. She'd got her scan appointment for four weeks, just before she was to see the consultant, and she supposed there was the slightest chance that they might find something operable.

It seemed highly unlikely, though, and clearly the consultant didn't think there was a great deal of hope.

Damn.

Connie sniffed hard. Her nose was running in the cold. So were her eyes. It must be the wind.

She sniffed again, scrubbing her nose on the back of her hand, and then finally she gave in, leaned against the trunk of a tree and howled.

*   *   *

'Connie?'

Patrick looked around, and found no sign of her. Surely she was back by now?

The dogs were missing, he realised, and it dawned on him that she might have taken them out for a walk.

'Is she here?' Edward said worriedly. 'She did come back, Daddy, didn't she? She promised.'

'Yes, she's back,' he said, noticing the missing coat and dog leads with a sigh of relief. He was right. 'She's walking the dogs. Shall we give her a surprise and order a Chinese take-away?'

Edward nodded. 'Can I have lemon chicken?'

He ruffled his son's hair. 'Sure. We'll order it now. Did you have a good day with Penny?'

He nodded. 'We did finger-painting. It was very messy,' he said, wide-eyed, and giggled. 'I made hand-prints all over my paper.'

'Have you got it to show me?'

He shook his little head. 'No. It was wet still. She said I can bring it next time. When can I go again?'

A success, Patrick thought, mildly surprised. 'Whenever you like. We'll talk to Connie about it, shall we?'

They phoned up for the take-away, then went in the car to fetch it, leaving a note for Connie on the kitchen table that said, 'Don't cook!'

They came back to find the dogs muddy and contented in their baskets, and Connie sitting at the table with her arm in her lap, sipping tea and looking a little forlorn.

'Connie!' Edward said with a cry of delight, and threw himself at her.

She put her tea down in the nick of time and hugged him, her hand cupping the back of his head and holding it hard against her shoulder. 'Hello, pumpkin. I missed you. Have you had a good day?'

'Brilliant. I did finger-painting.' He wriggled out of the hug and looked at her. 'How's your hand? Did you have the plaster off?'

'Yes, I did.'

'And is it better?'

She wrinkled up her nose, looking young and vulnerable and fragile. 'So-so. It feels very weird without the cast—all sort of bendy and tickly.'

'Oh. I 'spect you'll get used to it soon. We got a Chinese take-away.'

Patrick was busy unpacking the meal and taking the warmed plates out of the oven which he'd switched on before they'd gone out. He was watching Connie and Edward out of the corner of his eye, and his heart was full.

She seemed so sweet with him, so genuinely caring, and yet he could see she was hanging onto her control by a thread. He met her eyes over Edward's head, and she gave a tight little smile.

Later, it seemed to say.

They ate the meal, Patrick very conscious of Connie pushing food round on the plate, and then he took Edward up, bathed him and put him to bed.

'I want Connie to read me a story,' he said.

'Not tonight,' Patrick told him. 'Connie's tired out after her day. I think her arm's aching. Why don't I read you a story for a change?'

Edward nodded, quite happy with that. He snuggled down with Teddy Edward and by the time Patrick closed the book he was fast asleep.

Now for Connie, he thought.

She was still at the kitchen table, sitting there

amongst the litter of empty metal cartons, pushing a grain of rice round on the table with her left forefinger.

He scooped the debris off the table, gave it a quick wipe, poured her another glass of wine and sat down opposite.

'You were right,' she said without preamble, her voice hollow. 'The median nerve is damaged beyond repair. She's going to check with a scan, but it looks pretty grim.'

'Can I see?' he asked softly, and she laid the thin, pale little limb on the table. He pushed up her sleeve and studied it, turning it gently this way and that, looking at the scars, the range of movement, the weakness. Orthopaedically, he supposed, it was a success. Neurologically, though, it was a complete disaster.

'The skin's very dry—have you got any hand cream?'

'There's some over the sink,' she said woodenly.

He fetched it, smearing a generous dollop on the back of her wrist and working it carefully all round. Her arm lay in his hand, lifeless, a limb once so clever and responsive, so accurate, so deft. He smoothed it lovingly, pouring all his caring and tenderness into the touch. 'My poor Connie. Poor little arm,' he murmured gently under his breath, and then he felt her shake.

Very carefully, he put the arm down, went round and drew her to her feet, then led her through to the sitting room. Then he sat down, pulled her onto his lap and held her while she cried.

'Oh, Connie, I'm so sorry,' he murmured, tucking her hair behind her ears and wiping away the tears with his thumb.

She sniffed hard, rummaged in her pocket for a

soggy tissue and blew her nose. 'It could have been worse,' she said philosophically, scrubbing at the reddened tip. 'I could have killed myself falling. It was definitely the lesser of two evils.'

So brave, so silly. Such a waste.

She looked up into his eyes, and he saw a hunger in them that matched his own. 'Patrick?' she whispered.

She didn't need to ask twice. His heart was already drumming behind his ribs, and he thought if he didn't taste her soon he'd die.

She licked her lips, the tip of her tongue flicking out uncertainly to moisten them, and he gave a ragged groan and lowered his mouth to hers. Despite the raging fire inside him, he hardly touched her, his lips brushing hers softly, sipping, teasing, tormenting, until she cried out, a tiny whimper of need that undid him.

'Connie,' he whispered, and then there was no holding back, no teasing, just a wild hunger that wouldn't be satisfied.

He'd wanted to kiss her so much, for so long, and his imagination hadn't even begun to do her justice. His hand lay against her side and he moved it up, curling his thumb over the soft peak of her breast.

Her little cry was trapped in his mouth, and it made him bolder. He was so afraid to frighten her, to push her too hard in this fragile state, but then he remembered how tough she really was, how brave and determined and indomitable, and he forgot about being tame and gentle and taking it slowly.

His hand covered her breast completely, the fingers brushing against her ribs, the thumb lying in the soft shadow of her cleavage. She arched against him, begging for more, and he had to remind himself where they were.

'Edward,' he muttered, dragging his mouth from hers and hauling in lungfuls of air. His hand slid down to her waist, holding it tight. 'Connie, we can't.'

She went still, then her hand came up—her left hand, the strong one—and cupped his cheek.

'No, we can't. What a shame.'

He closed his eyes. He wanted her so much—not just for the physical reasons, but to hold her, to be close to her.

Dear God, he thought, I can't fall in love with her. I have Edward to consider now.

He dropped his head back against the wing of the chair and sighed. This was supposed to have been a cuddle for comfort, not a heavy petting session or a prelude to a wild affair.

He propped his head up again and looked down into her molten, honey-gold eyes. 'Are you OK? About the hand, I mean.'

She nodded. 'I suppose so. It was nothing I wasn't expecting. And, anyway, there's still a glimmer of hope, I suppose.'

'You could always go into general practice,' he suggested.

Connie laughed. 'You are kidding, aren't you? Tonsils one minute, cardiac arrest the next? You have to be a business manager as well as a physician, you need the constitution of an ox, the willing nature of a pack-horse and a brain like Einstein. No, thanks.'

He chuckled, diffusing the tension a little. 'I'm not sure if that was complimentary or not. I'm still working on it.'

'So am I,' she said, and laughed. Then her laugh

turned to a sigh. 'I was thinking of going back to paediatric medicine, but even for that I might not have enough motor control in my hand for things like putting in IV lines and so on, never mind writing up notes!'

'You could teach the other hand.'

She snorted. 'I'm not the slightest bit ambidextrous. I was finding it difficult in surgery, the amount I had to do with my left hand. I'm very definitely right-handed, to an almost absurd degree.'

'But you've survived without your right hand for weeks.'

'Just about.' She chuckled. 'I have to say it's the stupid, intimate little things you take for granted, like going to the loo, getting dressed, eating with a knife and fork. Such simple, everyday things, and they just become a nightmare. I haven't been able to wear anything with buttons or zips for ages, I can't tie laces— it's crazy!'

She went quiet, chewing her lip thoughtfully for a moment. 'I don't know what to do about my flat,' she said after a while. 'It's only rented, but it's in London and it's quite expensive to keep it going while I'm not there.'

'Why don't you wait until after the scan result?' he suggested. 'Just a little longer?'

'I suppose I could,' she agreed. 'It's only four weeks. It would be silly if they found they could relieve some pressure with a minor op and hey presto! Not that it's likely, but I buy lottery tickets every now and again. The odds probably are somewhat better.'

He chuckled, then patted her bottom. 'Come on, up you get. We need another glass of wine, and there's a programme on television I want to watch about general practices using co-operatives to cover their out-of-hours work. It might be quite interesting.'

She slid to her feet. 'I think, actually, I'll turn in. I'm tired. I'll go and have a long soak in the bath and then have an early night. Thanks for the Chinese.'

He stood up, cupped her shoulders in his hands and drew her against his chest, wrapping his arms around her and hugging her close. 'My pleasure, Connie. Sleep well. Wake me if you need anything.'

She nodded, went on tiptoe and pressed a quick kiss to his lips, then ran lightly up the stairs. Patrick followed her out, retrieved his glass and the bottle of wine from the kitchen and went back to watch his programme.

Funny. He couldn't seem to pay attention to it at all. All he could think about was the soft feel of Connie's breast under his hand, and the taste of her mouth, and the ache she was going to leave behind when she moved on like a ship in the night.

Because she would move on. She was a career doctor, and if and when her hand recovered enough, or even if it didn't, he was sure she would go back to London and leap back into the rat race.

And if and when he married again, it would be to a woman who wanted, above all, to be a mother. He'd made that mistake once before, and it had cost Edward dearly. He wouldn't make the same mistake again— and that meant not marrying Connie, no matter how much he was beginning to realise he might want to.

Suddenly it didn't bear thinking about.

'Connie?'

She looked up from her book, her heart leaping at the sight of Patrick, and felt a smile curve her lips before she could control it. 'Hi,' she said softly. 'Going out?'

'I'm going to see Tim Roberts. I thought you might like to come along for the ride, as Edward's at Penny's.'

She put the book down and got up, shuffling for her shoes and finger-combing her hair at the same time. 'Sure. I'm ready.'

He chuckled. 'Do you have any idea how refreshing that is?' he said wryly. 'Marina used to take two hours to get ready for the supermarket!'

Connie fell into step beside him. 'How long did you stay together?' she asked, amazed that it had been more than a few days—hours, even!

'Three years,' he told her. 'Edward was two and a half when she told me she wanted a divorce. I was more than ready to agree, but at the time I thought I'd get Edward.'

'And you didn't?'

He shrugged. 'She went for custody. The judge thought the mother at home was naturally better than the father who was out at work all day. Superficially it all sounds quite plausible, doesn't it? The fact is, Marina had a full-time nanny and spent all of her day in the beauty salon, shopping in Kensington or "doing lunch, dahling".'

His mimicry was wicked, and Connie chuckled despite the seriousness of the subject. 'So, in fact, there was no difference in the amount of time you could give him, just the amount of love?'

'Apparently,' he said, and slid behind the wheel, slamming the car door with unnecessary force. 'Anyway, it's all over now. He's with me, and if I have anything to say about it he won't ever spend another night under her roof.'

'Would the fact that you're still single make a difference to the judge if it goes back to court?'

He looked across the car at her, his face puzzled. 'You mean, would he consider it more favourably if I were married again? Possibly. Why?'

Connie shrugged. 'Just curious. I don't know how their minds work.'

'I think it depends on the judge. Ours was particularly blinkered. However.' He fired up the engine, dropped the car into gear and headed off towards Burnt House Farm and little Tim Roberts, thus ending the discussion. Connie let it drop. She didn't want to make him dredge up the messy details of his divorce, but she was curious as to what had influenced the judge to come to such an ill-advised conclusion.

Whatever. It was water under the bridge. What mattered now was that Edward was happy, and that Patrick had another chance with his son.

They pulled up outside the cream farmhouse, and Jackie Roberts opened the door to them with a smile. 'Hi, there. Come on in. Hello, Connie, how are you? How's the arm?'

'Oh, so-so,' Connie said, fielding the question. 'And how's Tim? Home, I gather. Is he better?'

'Oh, much,' Jackie said with a laugh. 'He's so bouncy I can hardly believe he was so sick. Come on through and see him.'

She was right, Connie thought, amazed at the change in the boy since she'd last seen him in a hospital bed a few short weeks ago. He was sitting in the kitchen, playing with a Game Boy, and he grinned as they came in.

'Auntie Connie!' he said, and looked past her to Patrick, frowning in concentration. 'Are you the doctor?' he asked, looking at his bag.

''Fraid so. Still, I've only come to check that you're both happy with being home. I'm going on another call nearby in a minute, so I thought I'd drop in. How is it now?'

Tim slid off the chair and stood up, hitching up his top and pulling down his tracksuit bottoms a little. 'Cool. I had a—lapa-something.'

'Laparotomy,' Patrick supplied helpfully. 'To discover the extent of the problem.'

'That's right. Well, whatever. Anyway, it's healed and I've got this cool scar now.'

So different, Patrick's eyes said as he shot her a smile. They didn't stay long. As he'd said, he had another call round the corner, but it was good to see a success story.

'Who next?' Connie asked him.

'Mother of five—says the baby's got earache. I'm visiting because I can't bear the thought of six of them descending on the surgery, and because I hate babies with earache. I feel so sorry for them and they always look so wretched.'

'Do you prescribe antibiotics?' she asked, curious as to how he treated under these conditions, because the current guidelines seemed to be only to use antibiotics in a life-and-death situation because of the threat of superbugs.

Patrick obviously didn't believe in that. 'Yes, for this, and for little children,' he said. 'I'm much tougher on adults, and encourage homeopathy and self-help remedies and patience, but with the littlies I just can't bring myself to be so mean,' he added with a grin.

They stopped outside a seedy, run-down little mid-terraced house in the country, with toys and sand and old bits of cars scattered all the way up the front garden to the door.

The woman opened it with one hand, a baby in the other, and let them in. They were straight into the main living room of the house, and there were three children lined up in front of the television, arguing about the channel, and another kicking a football against the back wall of the house. It bounced off the window, and Connie wondered how long it would be before the ball came through the glass.

'I'm Patrick Durrant, and this is Dr Wright,' Patrick said, introducing them. 'And this must be Letty.'

'That's right. It's her left ear,' the mother said, quite unnecessarily, because Letty was scrubbing at the ear with her arm and crying piteously.

'Let's have a look, then,' he suggested. 'If you could hold her on your lap with her bad ear facing outwards, I might be able to get a look... Yup, that's fine,' he said, after such a short glance that Connie wasn't sure he could possibly have seen anything. 'Yes, she's definitely got a nasty infection there, so I'll give her some antibiotic syrup—can you get that into her?'

The mother laughed. 'I expect so. I might have to sit on her, but I've done it a few times now with the others. I'm pretty slick.'

Connie chuckled. She'd seen some slick nurses on the wards in London, dealing with the little ones. Patrick wrote out the prescription and they left, giving a host of probably unnecessary advice, but given the state of the place and the unruly nature of the house-hold, Connie wasn't convinced the advice would be listened to.

As they were walking down the path, something flew through the air and landed in Patrick's hair.

'Oh, my word, what's that?' Connie said, and then started to laugh.

'What?' Patrick asked, a nervous edge to his voice. 'What is it?'

'Chewing gum,' she told him, chuckling. 'It's smothered. You'll have to cut it out.'

'I might not. You have to chill it with ice and crumble it, and then it's supposed to come out. I'll try that before I go to extremes.'

Connie laughed. From where she was standing there was no way that chewing gum was coming out without surgery, and she was looking forward to watching Patrick try and get it out by any other method.

'Disgusting little wretch,' he said with a sigh, getting into the car. 'Have we got any ice in the fridge?'

'I expect so. I'll have a look when we get in. Then I'll find the scissors for you.'

He shot her a dirty look and started the engine. 'Pessimist,' he growled.

She smiled with satisfaction. 'We'll see.'

She'd been right, of course. It annoyed Patrick to bits. She'd gone and collected Edward while he'd messed about with ice and made it worse, and then she'd come in and crowed victoriously, before producing the scissors.

'Here you go,' she said.

'No way! If you think it needs cutting out, you do it,' he told her.

'With my left hand?'

'If that's what it takes.'

She met his challenging stare for several seconds, then put the scissors in her left hand. 'God help you, then, because my nails on my right hand always look a complete mess. Right, are you ready?'

He nodded, and Edward shifted closer, fascinated.

She slid the scissors into the hair and caught the top of his ear, sticking the scissors into the little fold.

'Ouch!' he yelled. 'That was my ear!'

'Well, serves you right. You shouldn't have such sticky-out ears.'

Patrick poked his tongue out at her, then caught Edward's mesmerised expression. 'I've got sticky-out ears,' he told them. 'Mummy says they're like taxi doors, and I have to have an op'ration to shut them.'

Patrick felt a chill run through him. He was four years old—and if his hair hadn't been cut so ridiculously short, they wouldn't have shown!

'Nonsense,' he said, no longer worried about backing up Marina and presenting a solid front. He stuck his fingers under his hair and lifted it out of the way. 'My ears are just like yours—they're the best ears, trust me. They hear things other ears miss all the time.'

Edward's eyes widened. 'They're even bigger than mine!' he said, awestruck.

'Of course. That's because my head's bigger. My hands are bigger than yours as well, and my legs are longer. That's because you haven't finished growing.'

'I'm glad my legs aren't that long,' Edward said thoughtfully, studying his father with a quizzical expression, 'or I'd have to work in a circus!'

It was his first joke, and Connie and Patrick both laughed till their sides ached.

And the subject of the ears was closed, hopefully for ever.

CHAPTER SEVEN

IT HAD been a week since Patrick kissed Connie, since she'd come back from London and he'd held her and touched her with such tenderness.

Connie ached for him to do it again, to hold her again, to touch her like that once more with such unbearable gentleness.

Not that his kiss had been gentle, but she hadn't wanted it to be. No, the kiss had been fine the way it was. There just hadn't been any more of them, unfortunately.

Still, she and Edward were getting on well, and having lots of fun. They did more cooking, and then one day, when they'd made fairy cakes with Teddy Edward's help, Connie asked what they should do next.

'Could we take Teddy Edward on a picnic?' Edward asked. 'By the river? And catch minutes?'

Connie suppressed the smile. 'Minnows? I expect so. We might have a net somewhere in the back of the garage. I'll go and look. Why don't you put some fairy cakes in a little bag while I go and see?'

She found the net, and came back to discover Edward sitting in a sea of broken glass, tears streaming down his cheeks, white to the gills. 'Oh, pumpkin, what happened? Are you hurt?' She crouched beside him, hugging him, and he turned his head into her shoulder and wept.

'I broke a jamjar,' he sobbed. 'I'm sorry.'

She looked down at him, stroking his head and wiping away the tears. 'Is that all? You aren't hurt? Cut?'

The fair little head shook from side to side. 'No. I just broke it.'

'Well, if that's all, there's nothing to cry about! I'm always breaking things. It just happens, especially with this hard tiled floor. Just so long as you aren't hurt.'

She lifted him up, regretting the weakness of her right arm, and plonked him on the worktop while she swept the floor and cleared up all the glass. Then she found another jar, put it with the fairy cakes in a carrier bag and found a piece of string.

'What's that for?' he asked. 'Fishing?'

'No—to tie Teddy Edward to you, so neither of you can fall in the river and float away. All right?'

He grinned. 'Then he can catch me if I fall,' he said happily.

Not before I do, Connie thought, dodgy arm or not. I couldn't lose you, you're much too precious. 'Come on, then. We'll take the dogs—they like picnics, and we can have a bit of a party. We'll take them some biscuits.'

The dogs pricked their ears and sat up, making Edward laugh, and together they all headed off across the fields behind the house to the river where Connie had so often gone with Anthony. He'd taught her to catch minnows when she'd been no older than Edward, and it seemed right and yet very strange that she should be teaching this little one.

So much water under so many bridges, she thought, and so much of the water was so troubled.

'Can we sit here?' Edward asked, but it was a bit nettly so they moved along the back until they found a bit without nettles, and settled down there. Connie had brought a rug, and they spread it out, sat on the sides and put the picnic in the middle. That was where Patrick found them, using scraps of cake as bait to encourage the minnows to the surface so they could scoop them up with the net.

'Mind if I join you?' he asked, hunkering down beside Connie.

She couldn't have stopped the smile if her life had depended on it. 'Of course not. Have a fairy cake— we just made them.'

It was odd, she thought, how much more complete the party seemed with him there. 'How did you know where to find us?' she asked him as he stretched his long legs out beside her.

'I saw you all heading over the field from the surgery window. I was in the nurse's room, and as I'd just about finished, I watched to see which way you went, tidied up after the clinic and followed you.' He looked suddenly uncertain. 'Am I in the way?' he asked softly, so Edward wouldn't hear.

He was sitting on the edge of the bank, with Teddy Edward on his lap, talking to him about the fish. He was miles away, and utterly content. 'In whose way? I'm sure Edward's delighted to have you here, and I certainly don't mind.'

'Are you delighted to have me here?' he asked, a soft smile playing about his lips.

She was, but she wasn't falling for his obvious tactics so easily. 'Stop fishing,' she told him.

'I thought that was what it was all about.'

'Do I have to stop fishing?' Edward asked from the water's edge.

'No, sprog, you carry on. Connie's just teasing me.'

'OK.'

They watched his little head for a moment, bent to the bear's in earnest conversation, and Connie wondered how it must feel to know that you'd been responsible for the birth of something as amazing as that funny little boy.

All of a sudden she felt a great wave of love and tenderness, and a terrible yearning ache for him to be hers, and for there to be others, hers and Patrick's. She jumped to her feet.

'I'm going to take the dogs for a little stretch,' she told him. 'You stay here with Edward, could you? Thanks.' And whistling up the dogs who were watching the fairy cakes with enormous enthusiasm, she set off up the path beside the river.

It was all too much. Living with Patrick all the time, it was very bitter sweet, and she wondered if she was just torturing herself by staying up here or if she shouldn't just go back to London and wait for her arm to heal.

No. She couldn't do that. She'd done it for weeks after her arm was broken, and she'd gone stir crazy. That was why she'd gone to Yorkshire.

Perhaps she should go backpacking again?

She sighed. No. She couldn't do that. She was needed here, at least for a little longer, and the next few weeks would pass much faster if she was here with them.

'Penny for 'em.'

She jumped and whirled round, her hand on her heart. 'Where's Edward?' she asked, immediately concerned.

'He's coming. He says the fish are tired and they've gone to lie down, so he and Teddy Edward are eating the last of the fairy cakes and packing up. I said I'd come and get you—and, don't worry, I've pulled the blanket away from the edge of the water and told him to be careful. And, anyway, don't change the subject.'

'What subject?' she asked, confused.

He smiled gently and cupped her cheek. 'Whatever it is that was making you look so forlorn.'

'Oh. That subject,' she said, flannelling.

'Is it your arm?' he asked, his face concerned.

She nodded. 'Sort of, in a way. It's not knowing. It's the waiting, being in limbo. I'm not very good at it.'

'Nor am I,' he said with a sigh, turning back towards Edward. 'I saw another practice advertised the other day, but it was nothing like as good as this. They all seem to be in a horrible area, or else they're part of a busy group practice, or it's part time, or there's some other fatal flaw.'

'Do you want a single-handed practice, then?' she asked. 'I thought most people these days liked to be in a group.'

He shrugged. 'Maybe. I don't know. I like working alone and being my own boss, and, with a co-operative doing the out of hours stuff most of the time, it's not as tiring as it used to be in the old days. I have to say if I had to design a practice that suited me ideally, it would be this one, but it's not available so there's no point in fretting about it.'

They arrived back at the picnic site, to find Edward and the bear curled up together on the rug, having a nap. 'He must have been tired,' Connie said softly. 'He'll get chilled if he stays there—the ground's too damp to lie on.'

'I'll carry him if you can manage the rest,' Patrick suggested, and scooping up the child and bear—still

tied together with the piece of string—he waited for
Connie to pick up all the other things, then they
headed back over the fields to the house.

'I'll put him on the sofa,' he murmured, and Connie
put the kettle on. Moments later he was back, phone
messages in hand.

'That's what you get for snatching a few minutes.
I have to go out before surgery—urgent visit. I'll see
you soon.'

He waggled his fingers and went, and she thought,
if we were married, he would have kissed me, and she
felt a great wave of loneliness.

Which was ridiculous, because they weren't married—they weren't even close. So he'd kissed her
once. Clearly he thought it had been a mistake because
he hadn't done it again.

She made herself a cup of tea, took it in the sitting
room and vowed to do her physiotherapy until Edward
woke up.

'Connie, have you got a minute?'

'Sure.' She flicked a glance at Edward, still fast
asleep, and went out quietly after Patrick. 'What's the
matter?' she asked him once they were out of earshot.

'One of the patients—Mrs Grimwade. I believe you
know her?'

'Yes, she used to run the village shop. She's amazing. What about her?'

'She's had a stroke—a few days ago, by all ac-
counts, but she's refused to tell anybody because she
knows she'll have to go to hospital. Her neighbour's
been looking after her, and she called me in because
she was so worried. Of course, Mrs Grimwade's cross

about it, but she's still refusing to go to hospital because of her kittens.'

'Kittens? Again?'

He nodded. 'Apparently she was brought these three kittens when their mother was run over—they're about fifteen weeks now, but she's been hand-rearing them from ten days, and she's besotted by them and can't bear to leave them. I just wondered if you'd got any influence or if you knew anyone who'd have the litter so she didn't have to worry.'

Connie laughed. 'Oh, she'll worry, whatever. She adores cats. Hasn't she got any others at the moment?'

He shook his head. 'Apparently not. Just the kittens. Connie, she's got to go to hospital. She's in urgent need of anticoagulation therapy before she has another stroke or a heart attack, and I can't allow these kittens to get in the way of her life.'

'I think she'd disagree with you.'

He remembered the argument and laughed. 'She *did* disagree with me. That's why I've come to get your help. She said you'd understand.'

Connie snorted. 'Oh, yes, I understand. I've done just the same thing in the past—well, my mother has. In fact, my mother was saying the other day that they ought to get another cat once Dad comes home.'

Patrick looked at her narrowly. 'Another? As in, A. N. Other? One? Not three!'

She chuckled. 'No, probably not three, but we've had three in the past—and, anyway, if they're fifteen weeks they're over the worst. They'll be litter trained and old enough to go out in the garden, and Edward would simply love them.'

Another thing to tear them both away from, Patrick

thought despairingly. Unless one of the kittens was Edward's, and came with them when they moved?

'Do you think she'd let you have them?'

A warm, lovely chuckle bubbled Connie's throat. 'Oh, yes. I know she will, just as she knows I'll take them. Besides, stroking cats is very good therapy, and I can practise my physio by tickling their ears with each finger in turn. What colour are they?'

He laughed. 'What possible difference could that make?'

'You're right, it makes none. I was just curious. So, what are they?'

Patrick shook his head, bemused. 'I don't know— tabby? Black? I couldn't be sure, they were moving too fast.'

'Lively, are they?'

He rolled his eyes. 'I have surgery shortly. If you want these cats and you think it'll be all right with your parents and it will get Mrs Grimwade into hospital, then let's, for goodness' sake, go for it!'

'We'll take Edward,' Connie said. 'He'll love it— and we can take the cat carrier. It's in the garage. We'll need to stop at the village shop for cat litter and food—'

'All right, all right. Come on,' he chivvied, one eye on the time, and went and woke Edward.

He came, sleepy and bleary and fascinated, and chattered excitedly between yawns all the way there.

The house was chilly when they got there, and Connie was instantly worried about the poor woman. She was slumped in a chair, the left side of her face drooping, her left hand curled into a little claw. There was a definite aroma of incontinence in the air, and the place was a mess.

'Mrs Grimwade!' Connie exclaimed, going up to her and taking her frail, gnarled old hands. She used both hands, Patrick noticed, and wondered if she'd realised. 'I gather you're very poorly—I am sorry,' she said, her voice rich with sympathy. She crouched down beside the elderly woman and patted her knee.

'Patrick tells me you're worried about the kittens. Well, you mustn't because, if you'll let me, I'll take them. My parents were talking just the other day about getting some more cats, and I know they'd be delighted if they were yours again.'

'Again?' Patrick said, and Connie flashed him a smile.

'Oh, yes. Our cats always come from Mrs Grimwade, don't they?'

'Have done in the past. Oh, Connie, you don't know how relieved I'd be. I never meant to keep them all, but nobody seemed to want kittens this summer. They're such lovely little chaps, too—all boys. The tabby with the circle on his side is Leo, the other tabby's Joey and the bad little black one is Mickey. The boy's made friends all ready, look.'

They looked, and found Edward on the floor, two kittens fighting with his shoelaces, the other one on his lap attacking a bit of string he was dangling.

'Right, let's put them in the cat carrier and take them home, and we can get you off to hospital,' Patrick said firmly. While Connie and Edward rounded up the kittens, he contacted the hospital, arranged admission and knocked on the neighbour's door to tell her what was happening.

They got back to the surgery just before the patients started arriving, and because they hadn't had time to go shopping Connie and Edward shut the kittens in the kitchen, put the dogs in the hall and walked to the shop.

It was a long way back with the cat litter, which was heavy, clay-based granules, and Connie was beginning to wonder what had possessed her by the time they got home.

'Right, let's feed them and make them a bed,' Connie suggested, 'and perhaps they ought to meet the dogs.'

That was amusing but not very eventful, if you didn't count Mickey walking up to Toby and smacking him on the nose. 'Poor Toby,' Connie said, trying not to laugh at the sight of the big dog seen off by the kitten.

Mickey then jumped onto the worktop, leapt across the gap towards Connie who was washing up the food bowls and slithered all the way down the front of the kitchen cupboards, claws screeching, to land in an embarrassed heap.

'Lost your wings, Icarus?' Connie said, laughing, then added, 'He should have been called that instead.' Then she told Edward the ancient Greek story of Icarus and the wings that fell off when he tried to fly to the sun and it melted the wax that held them.

'That's silly,' Edward said with a laugh. 'He should have used proper glue.'

Connie explained that proper glue hadn't been invented, but Edward had lost interest in the legendary Icarus. He was much more interested in the feline version. 'Can we call him Icki instead of Mickey?' he asked, and she shrugged.

'I don't see why not. What do you think of that, Icki? Want to be called Icarus?'

The kitten said, 'Mreouw.' Then it sat down in the middle of the kitchen floor, and proceeded to wash.

'I think that's a yes,' Connie said with a laugh. 'Don't you?'

It was after surgery, while Patrick was out on a call and Edward was entertaining the kittens in the kitchen, that Connie heard a frantic pounding on the surgery door.

All the practice staff had gone home and Patrick was out. Connie debated ignoring it, but only for a second. There was something so urgent, so terrified about that pounding that she told Edward to stay where he was and ran through to the surgery.

It was dark, but in the light from the hall she could see a young woman, holding a little child. The outside door was locked, but she had grabbed the keys as a reflex and now quickly opened the door.

'What's the matter?' she asked, quickly taking in the child's condition. She was drooling on her mother's shoulder, her breath was rasping and she had a nasty blue colour. 'What do you think is wrong?'

'She's been feverish this afternoon, and I thought she was getting a cold or flu—then suddenly she started to breath really loudly, and she couldn't seem to get her breath. She can't breathe if she lies down, and I tried steaming her but it didn't seem to help. Then I noticed she was going blue, and I didn't know what to do!'

She ground to a halt, fighting back tears and panic, and Connie studied the child without touching her. 'You say it's been getting slowly worse over the afternoon?'

'Yes. She was fine this morning.'

Connie nodded. 'OK, Dr Durrant's out at the moment, but what I'm going to do is call an ambulance immediately and arrange for a doctor to come out with it. She might only have croup, but she might have a condition called epiglottitis, and if she has, I want her in hospital fast so they can get a tube in and start to treat her.'

The mother looked fearful. 'Are you sure? Shouldn't we wait for Dr Durrant?'

'No,' she said firmly. 'I do know what I'm talking about. I'm a paediatrician, and I've seen this before. I could examine her throat, but the danger with that is that the epiglottis suddenly obstructs the airway, and she could suffocate.'

'Oh, my God,' the mother said, just as the child started to gasp and struggle in her arms.

Oh, no, Connie thought. Not now, please. Let me get help. Patrick, come back. I can't do this, not with one hand!

'Help her!' the woman cried. 'Do something. Please! She's choking to death!'

Connie hesitated just a moment longer, then ushered them through to the nurse's room, flicking on the lights. 'Lay her on there, and put these gloves on. I'm going to tell you what to do.'

'Me!' the woman wailed. 'I can't! You'll have to! Why can't you do it? I'll kill her. You're a doctor, aren't you?'

'Yes, but…' She looked at the little girl, now limp and blue on the treatment couch, and realised there was no time to fiddle about or teach anyone anything. The child was going to die anyway if she didn't do something. So she'd be struck off if it went wrong. So what? She didn't have a career left to protect!

She opened the sterile pack with a scalpel in it, swabbed the child's neck, and felt carefully for the membrane between the thyroid and cricoid cartilages in the neck. Then, sending up a quick one for a little guidance for her wrong hand, she stroked down the throat over the membrane, pierced the space and inserted the handle, twisting it to open the hole.

They heard air rushing in, and the child's colour improved within moments.

The mother, not unnaturally, began to cry, and Connie thought her legs were going to give way.

'Hold this,' she told the woman, 'and don't move it. I'm going to find a tube.'

She fumbled one-handed for a catheter, cut the end off it, took the scalpel out and pushed the soft plastic tube into the hole. 'There. Now I need tape. Can you find me some in that drawer, and cut me off some strips about so long?'

She held up her right hand and forced her fingers and thumb to splay. They didn't go very far, so the tape was a bit short, but it did the job and soon the tube was secure.

Then she heard firm, masculine footsteps striding down the corridor.

'Connie?'

The door opened, and she turned round and summoned up a weak and slightly hysterical smile. 'Hello, Patrick. Would you like to take over? I've just done a laryngotomy—perhaps you'd like to check it out?'

And she sat down in the nearest chair with a plop, and watched him go smoothly into action. He took one look at the mother, weeping in the corner, then asked Connie about the child's symptoms, what had prompted the emergency airway and if they'd contacted the hospital yet.

'With my free hand?' she said, a little frantically.

'OK. Could you do that now? I want to set up a drip. Oh, and, Connie?' he said as she was leaving the room. 'Well done.'

They sat down that night to a celebratory glass of wine. At least, Patrick said it was to celebrate. Connie reckoned it was to steady her still shaky nerves. She'd phoned the hospital, gone back and helped Patrick, soothed the mother while they waited, and in between times she'd run in and out, checking up on Edward.

He, of course, hadn't gone anywhere. He'd simply sat on the kitchen floor, playing with the kittens and having a wonderful time, quite oblivious to the drama being played out at the other end of the house.

Now, though, Edward was in bed, the kittens were sleeping in their box in the corner of the kitchen, the dogs were stretched out in front of the fire Patrick had lit and Connie had finally stopped shaking.

'To think I used to operate on babies of thirty weeks' gestation!' she said with a wobbly laugh. 'I nearly had a pink fit when I realised what I was going to have to do.'

'But you did it,' Patrick said, from the other end of the sofa. 'That's what matters.'

'But it wasn't good—and my other hand was totally useless. Unless this scan in two weeks comes up with something stunning, that might be the last operation I ever perform—and, judging by the way I reacted, it might be just as well!'

Patrick chuckled. 'Silly girl. I would have been

shaky, doing something like that. It's the adrenaline rush.'

'Hmm,' she grunted. 'Well, I've decided I don't like adrenaline. Maybe I'll take up flower-arranging—can I do that with one hand?'

'You haven't got just one hand. You've got two, and in time you'll remember that. Did you know you held Mrs Grimwade's hands with both of yours?'

She was surprised. 'Did I?' she asked, struggling to remember. 'I didn't notice.'

'And that's a good sign. Isn't it?' he prompted.

She smiled. 'Yes, Patrick, it's a good sign.' She put her wineglass down and looked across at him. 'Patrick?'

'Mmm?'

'I could use a hug,' she said in a low voice.

He put his glass down and held out his arms, and she scooted along the sofa into them. 'Oh, Connie,' he said softly, and his arms closed around her, holding her firmly against his heart. She laid her right hand on his chest, feeling the steady beat, and it seemed to breathe life into the damaged nerves.

Her hand felt suddenly warmer, more comfortable— safer. So did she. She snuggled up closer, sighing softly, and let the warmth and comfort of his arms soak into her.

He seemed to go still, then she felt the tension in him wind a little tighter.

'Connie?' he murmured.

She lifted her head and met his eyes, and knew he was going to kiss her again. She smiled, just a tiny, feather-soft ghost of a smile, and moved so she was facing him, her side lying across his lap. Then she reached up with her arms and drew him down, lifting her lips to his.

Heat seared between them, and yet the kiss was curiously gentle and almost chaste. His hands didn't move, nor did hers, and yet Connie knew she had never been kissed like this before. It was as if he touched the bottom of her soul, and she touched his.

I love you, she wanted to say, but she had to bite back the words. She could only show him, so she did, her hand threading into his hair, sifting the silky strands, drawing him closer.

A low rumble erupted from his throat and he shifted so that his body lay along the sofa next to hers. His arms were round her, holding her against his chest, and his mouth came down again and took hers.

She would have given him anything, but he asked for nothing, only her mouth, so very willing under his, and the feel of her body so taut with need she thought it would snap.

She could feel the pressure of his arousal against her hip, and he groaned and moved so that they lay aligned in a strangely innocent intimacy.

'Connie,' he whispered against her throat, and she held him, aching for him, and knew that he would never be hers.

He was going away, and she was going to London, and it was all too complicated for her to bear.

'Just kiss me,' she pleaded, and his mouth found hers again, his lips gentle now, not demanding but giving, comforting, and she tasted the salt of his tears on her lips. 'Patrick?'

'Don't talk. Just hold me,' he said gruffly, and she wrapped her arms tightly round him, squeezed her eyes shut and hung on for dear life.

CHAPTER EIGHT

CONNIE awoke to a fire burned down to ashes, a rug snuggled round her to keep her warm and no sign of Patrick.

She peered at her watch in the dim morning light that came through the chink in the curtains. Nearly seven! She was stunned. She'd slept all night, as warm as toast thanks to Patrick, and the only reason she was awake now was the soft footfall overhead and the sound of running water.

The dogs yawned and stretched and wagged their tails, and she suddenly remembered the kittens and flew off the sofa, almost falling over the trailing end of the blanket in her haste.

They were fine, of course. Starving hungry as young things always were when they woke up, and full of the joys of spring. She put the dogs out, opened another tin of kitten food, dealt with the litter tray and let the dogs back inside, all while the kettle was coming to the boil.

Not bad, she thought, for a one-handed cripple. Once the kittens had all had a cuddle and the dogs had been fussed over, too, she poured two mugs of tea and carried them both in her left hand, letting herself out and fending off the kittens with the other.

Connie rolled her eyes as Icki escaped yet again. 'I'm sure all our other kittens weren't this bad,' she told him, firmly removing him from the sitting room and scooting him back through the kitchen doorway.

They probably had been, but she didn't remember. She carried the tea, now slopped all over her hand, up to Patrick and knocked on his door. He opened it, clad only in a towel and the remains of his shower water, and took the mug from her with a sigh.

'Lifesaver. That was my next job. How are you?'

'Fine.' She smiled up at him, unable to quell the warm, squishy feeling inside that she got just from looking at him. 'Thanks for putting the rug round me.'

'Any time. I couldn't bear to leave you, but I didn't want Edward to wake in the night and not be able to find me.'

'And did he?'

He shook his head. 'No. He's still asleep. Come in and drink your tea.'

She was tempted. Oh, boy, was she tempted, but she backed away, shaking her head. 'No, I mustn't. I need to shower and get ready. I'm going to town with Edward to get him new shoes, and we need to find a toy for the kittens.'

His smile called her a liar, but he didn't stop her. 'See you in a minute,' he said, and made it sound like a promise.

She went into her room, closed her door and leaned against it. She'd been so close to him last night—too close, really, for her sanity. Still, it seemed she had no choice. He'd needed her, and she'd been powerless to turn him away. Besides, nothing had happened.

Nothing except a meeting of two lonely, isolated souls, each with a whole host of problems.

'Oh, Patrick,' she murmured, slithering down the door to sit cross-legged at the foot, her eyes slightly out of focus, her brain even more so.

'Connie? Fancy a cooked breakfast?'

She leapt up, slopping tea all over herself, and grabbed the doorhandle, whipping the door open. 'Sounds good,' she said brightly. 'I'll just have a quick shower and I'll be down.'

She went into the bathroom, still steamy and smelling of Patrick's aftershave, and scrubbed the mirror with her sleeve. She even *looked* daft this morning. She washed as quickly as she could with the wrong hand, and then had to struggle to clean her teeth.

Crazy, how such a simple task could assume such an absurdly frustrating importance. 'They're teeth,' she told herself crossly out loud. 'Just teeth. You're not scrubbing them for an operation or a film, only so they don't fall out. They don't need to be surgically sterile! It really doesn't matter if you can't do it properly with that hand.'

She dressed and went downstairs, to find Patrick up to his neck in kittens on the kitchen floor, Edward beside him, both having a wonderful time. He looked up and smiled at her, a welcome in his eyes that warmed her to the cockles of her heart—wherever they were.

'I wonder how Mrs Grimwade is,' she said, stepping over them all carefully and resisting the urge to bend down and hug them, cats and all. 'I expect she's worrying about these babies.'

Patrick snorted. 'She needn't. They're going to be spoilt to death, I can tell. We aren't, though. I haven't done a thing for breakfast yet—I've been otherwise engaged.' His grin was wry.

'It's only what I expected,' she grumbled with a smile. 'So, have you still got time to cook before surgery, or should I stick in some toast?'

He smiled apologetically. 'Toast, I think. I'm sorry. I got you up under false pretences.'

'We're going to the shops,' Edward announced, 'to buy shoes.'

Patrick stood up and dusted himself off. 'And I,' he said wryly, 'am going to change into a clean pair of trousers. See you in a minute.'

While his son was being shopped for and entertained by Connie, Patrick took his morning surgery and went out on his visits.

He was finding it hard to concentrate, his mind constantly going back to Connie and the few all-too-short hours he'd spent in her arms. He'd wanted more. They both had, but common sense had prevailed, helped by the knowledge that Edward had been there and quite likely to wake up.

It was probably just as well. He had to find another practice, and it was looking increasingly likely that he was going to have to move some distance from London—too far, certainly, to sustain their relationship once she returned.

There was a practice in Devon, a husband-and-wife team, who were looking for a new partner since the wife had become pregnant with twins. It looked hopeful. He was going to ring later and talk to them.

For now, though, he had the joys of Mrs Pike, newly returned from hospital, and her hip replacement. He pulled into the drive and rang the doorbell, and was greeted by the younger Mrs Pike, accompanied by a wall of noise from her mother-in-law's television.

'Morning,' he said with a smile. 'How is she?'

'Oh, in fine form,' the woman said, rolling her eyes,

but she looked less run down and depressed than she had.

'Enjoy your break?'

'I can't tell you how much. I hadn't realised how much it was getting to me.'

He hesitated in the hall. 'Have you thought that it might be time for her to have more specialist care?'

'You mean put her in a home? My husband wouldn't hear of it.'

'But if there comes a time when you can't manage? What if looking after her makes you ill?'

She shrugged. 'I'm strong enough. She drives me potty, but I dare say I can cope for another year or so.'

'And what if she lives to be a hundred?'

Mrs Pike seemed to blanch. 'You think that's likely?'

'I don't know. It happens. Statistically, the older you get, the greater the likelihood of you reaching that age.'

'Then I suppose I shall just have to deal with it,' Mrs Pike said. 'She wouldn't be happy in a home and, anyway, I'm used to her ways. It's not so bad. It's the telly that drives us crazy, on so loud.'

Patrick nodded, then had an idea. 'You know you can get headphones—cordless ones, so she could listen to it with the volume off?'

Mrs Pike brightened visibly. 'You can? I think that would make all the difference, you know. It's that constant noise. Do you have to have a special set?'

He shook his head. 'I don't think so. It needs the right kind of socket for the transmitter, but most televisions these days have them. If it's a newish set you should be all right.'

'I'll look into it,' Mrs Pike said enthusiastically. 'Come and see her, anyway. She's looking good.'

They followed the sound of the chat-show host's voice up the hall and into the elderly lady's room. She was sitting in her chair, haranguing the unsuspecting host and his guest, and she jumped when she saw them.

'Ann, you've got to stop creeping up on me like that!' she said crossly. 'You'll give me a heart attack one day. And why are you here, young man? Come to tell me I'm going to be crippled, have you?'

Ann Pike turned off the television and Patrick's ears sighed with relief. 'Not at all. Your daughter-in-law tells me you're doing really well. How do you feel?'

'Oh—well, up and down. I'm not sure they've done it right, you know. They said I can't turn and I can't cross my legs and I can't bend over and I can't do this and that—I reckon they know they've made a mistake and they're just hoping I'll die before I find out!'

Patrick chuckled. 'It's just to give the muscles time to recover and grow strong again, so they hold the new joint properly in position,' he yelled. 'Let's have a look at you.'

He examined her quickly, found everything to be well and then sat down next to her and took her hand. 'Mrs Pike, I'm going to ask the community physio-therapist to come and see you, and give you some exercises to do with her and with your daughter-in-law, and then I think you'll find you'll be back to normal and right as rain in no time. Now the other thing is, have you ever thought of having a hearing aid?'

'A what?'

'A hearing aid,' he yelled.

She flapped her hand. 'Why would I want one of them? I can hear perfectly well!'

Patrick stood up. He knew when he was beaten. 'I'll get the physio to call,' he told her, and turned to Ann. 'I'll let myself out. Give me a ring if you've got any problems.'

He did a few more visits, then went back to the surgery, found the professional journal with the Devon practice advert in it, and dialled the number. Within ten minutes he'd set up an interview at the weekend, got directions and arranged for someone else to cover the out-of-hours commitment he had on Sunday afternoon. That would give him nearly thirty-six hours to drive down, meet them, look around and get back.

All he had to do now was ask Connie to have Edward.

'Sure.' Connie tried to smile, but—Devon! It was so far. It seemed further than Yorkshire, because London was in the way and it meant grappling with the M25. Of course, once she was back in London it was only the M4 and M5 so it wouldn't be quite so bad, but it was still too far. Oh, Lord, she thought, I'm going to have to say goodbye to them both, and she swallowed a lump in her throat.

'I want to get away the minute I can after surgery on Saturday—probably about ten-thirty, if I can manage it—and I'll try and get back before you go to bed on Sunday so I can tell you all about it.'

Connie wasn't at all sure she wanted to hear. Unless, of course, it was hopeless, like the one in Yorkshire. That would be all right.

'Don't rush,' she advised him. 'Make sure you've seen everything you need to see.'

All the pitfalls, the nooks and crannies, the skeletons in the closet. With any luck the wife will hate you and the husband is so besotted he won't be able to deny her.

Fat chance. Nobody was going to hate him. Oh, damn and blast.

'Can we let the kittens out?' Edward asked, tugging at her sleeve. She latched onto the distraction like a drowning man clutching at straws. Anything rather than think about Patrick going.

'No, sweetheart, not for a few more days. They need to feel safe in the house before they go out, or they might not come back if they get frightened, and we wouldn't want to lose any of them, would we?'

He looked crestfallen. 'I tell you what,' she suggested brightly. 'After we've all had lunch, why don't you take them up to your bedroom for a little while? They could play up there, and as long as we take up the litter tray, we shouldn't have any little accidents. Now, what shall we have for lunch?'

'Chocolate crispy cakes,' Edward said promptly.

'I'll second that.'

Connie shook her head in despair. 'I thought you were supposed to set a nutritional example to your son and your patients?' she said with a laugh. 'How about beans on toast, and yoghurt for pudding?'

'Can I have strawberry?'

She ruffled Edward's hair. 'I expect so, if there's one left.'

She didn't have to struggle with the can opener because the baked beans had a ring-pull, but that was difficult enough. Patrick put in the toast, Edward laid the table with the knives and forks the wrong way round, and Connie stirred the beans vigorously and thought how much she was going to miss them.

'Are you supposed to be mashing them?' Patrick asked softly in her ear, and his arms came round her, one hand taking the handle of the pan, the other the wooden spoon, trapping her against the edge of the cooker.

His body was lean and hard against hers, and he groaned softly under his breath and nudged his hips against her.

Oh, Lord.

She grabbed the spoon back. 'They're sticking on the pan,' she said, pushing him out of the way with her bottom. Unfortunately it brought her firmly up against him, and he groaned again.

'I love your sassy little bottom,' he murmured in her ear, so softly she could hardly hear it but just loud enough to make her heart go loopy.

'Patrick,' she warned under her breath, and he laughed and moved away.

'OK, sport, shall we get some glasses of water?' he said to Edward, and then held him up at the sink while he turned the tap on full and drenched them both.

'That'll cool you off,' Connie said cheerfully, and wondered if they'd think she was completely mad if she stuck her head under the tap!

It *was* a long way to Devon. Patrick followed the A12, the M25, the M4, the M5 and then turned off just after Taunton to head along the north Devon coast road. It took five hours to the last motorway junction, and another hour along the winding minor roads to the practice itself.

The scenery, though, was spectacular for the last

hour, and Patrick knew he would like living there. At least, until he'd met Connie, he would have liked it.

Now it just seemed a very long way from her.

He pulled up outside the practice at four-thirty, and was met by a cheerful man in his late thirties, with slightly receding hair and sparkling blue eyes. 'Good to see you—how was the journey?' he asked, pumping Patrick's hand, and led him into the surgery.

'Cup of tea? Cloakroom? Guided tour?'

Patrick laughed. 'All of them. I'll start with the cloakroom.'

It was an interesting afternoon. He spent two hours at the practice talking to Mike Bryant, then went back to the Bryants' house and met Jane, already visibly pregnant and struggling with another youngster. They had supper, and when Patrick said he thought he ought to go and find a local hostelry for the night, they wouldn't hear of it.

'But surely you're staying!' Jane exclaimed. 'You can't come all that way and not stay the night with us! Besides, you might have all sorts of awful habits and we need a chance to find out about them.'

'So you want to interview me in my sleep?' he said with a laugh, and gave in. 'Thank you. That would be very kind, if you really mean it.'

'Then tomorrow if you've got time you can come on some calls with me and see the area,' Mike suggested. 'I have to pop into the cottage hospital now— you can come and do that as well, if you like. See the set-up and so forth.'

So he went to the hospital, run by the local GPs and staffed by a fleet of cheerful nurses who knew most of the patients, and helped with a young lad who'd discovered booze and was somewhat the worse for wear, and then they went back to the house to find that Mike had another call to go on.

'You stay here and get your head down,' Mike advised. 'You've got a long drive tomorrow. Jane'll make you a drink, won't you, darling?'

'Of course. Go on, I can manage. I can tell him all the horror stories.'

She did no such thing, but it was clear they'd found both of them working covering the on-call very demanding of their personal time, and she would be happy to sit back now and be a mother.

He went to bed convinced that they were both lovely people, probably people he could work with, and almost convinced that if they offered him the partnership he would take it.

In the morning Mike showed him more of the glorious Devon countryside, cheerfully confessing that it was a deliberate ploy to sell the area to him, and Patrick had to admit it worked. In the mid-October sunshine, with the autumn leaves turning gold in the combes and the ponies grazing on the moorland, it was a very special place.

They went back to the house after his calls, and as Patrick was about to leave, Mike said, 'I want to take a week to think about it, and I want you to as well. Then we'll talk, but I think we've got a lot to talk about.'

Patrick nodded. 'Yes, I agree. It's a beautiful place. It's the sort of place I could bring up my son without a qualm. It's all the other things that need considering. It's a big step—it has to be the right one for all of us.'

Mike smiled and stuck out his hand. 'I agree. Let's hope we all come to the same conclusion. Safe journey.'

'Thanks. And thank Jane for me again, would you, for her hospitality?' Patrick released Mike's hand, got into the car and drove off. As he glanced in the rear-view mirror, Mike lifted his hand in a wave.

Such friendly, decent people. A practice set-up he could work with and understand. A little community hospital, albeit under threat, but still there, a wonderful resource for the patients and doctors alike.

Oh, yes, it had everything.

Except Connie.

There was an accident on the motorway on the way home, and Patrick stopped to help. It was a multiple pile-up in perfectly reasonable weather conditions, caused because people just simply had to drive too close together and too fast to take avoiding action.

The accident had only just happened, and Patrick's first clue was a police car flying past, with lights and siren going. Then there was another one, and the traffic started to slow. After ten minutes of queueing, he arrived at the scene and pulled over without hesitation.

A policeman tried to wave him on, but he took his bag out of the car and ran towards the crashed vehicles. The policeman gave him the thumbs-up, and he spoke to the man's colleague beside the cars.

'I'm a doctor—do you need me?'

The policeman's face cleared. 'Do we ever, Doc. There's a young couple in the first car, but I don't think they're badly hurt. They had a blow-out. The next car's got a young family in it, and I think some of them need attention. The third car seems OK, just shaken up, and then the rest I haven't had time to check.'

He nodded. 'I'll do some triage and see what I can do.'

He ran first to the front car, but the policeman had been right. The couple were whiplashed, and he advised them to stay there until the ambulance arrived and put collars on them. 'Don't move too much,' he instructed.

Then he ran to the second car, and found the father's legs wedged under the crumpled dash, blood oozing from his thigh and from cuts on his face from impacting the steering-wheel. The mother was frantically trying to keep calm, but the children were in hysterics in the back and she was rapidly joining in.

'It's all right, I'm a doctor,' he told her, and she dissolved into tears.

'Oh, thank God. You've got to help him. He's going to die.'

'No, he isn't. He's going to hurt for a while, but he'll be all right,' Patrick assured her, checking the man's pulse as he spoke.

'Where do you hurt?' he asked him.

'Leg, head, shoulder,' he mumbled. 'My leg especially.'

'Can you move them at all?'

He stirred, moaning softly, and Patrick told him to keep still and the ambulance men would be with him shortly. The children seemed all right but, like toddlers everywhere, they were too small to explain anything to and too old to not notice.

'Why don't you get in the back with them?' Patrick suggested to the woman. 'Your husband will be all right. I think the children need you, if you're OK.'

She nodded and crawled through the space between the seats. Immediately the children started to settle, and after checking them quickly, Patrick moved on, hailing a policeman and asking him to get the fire brigade to cut the driver out.

In the next car the driver was just shocked, and in the fourth there were no injuries. He was just about to check the next when a policeman hailed him.

'Here, Doc! Casualties for you.'

The last car seemed to have hit the others with more force and, of the two occupants, he found one already dead, the other bleeding copiously from a head wound. On examination he found the skull compressed, and he didn't hold out much hope.

An ambulance arrived, and he sent them straight to the last car for the surviving occupant. There was nothing Patrick himself could do. The man needed urgent skull decompression in hospital, scans, brain-stem tests, transfusions.

All he could do by the side of the road was assess and direct, and put on sticking plasters, effectively. However, at least it saved time when the crews arrived. There was only one other car, the one he hadn't checked, so he went to look inside.

A young woman with a baby in the back seat was slumped unconscious over the wheel. The baby was crying vigorously, probably unharmed, but there was a dog howling in the back and when Patrick looked in he found it had been horribly injured.

'We need a vet—dog here needs urgent attention,' he told the policeman. 'And this woman needs to get to hospital fast. She's unconscious with a head injury—it might be minor, but I doubt it. Oh, and the baby in the back looks fine.'

He stayed until the rescue looked well under way and there was nothing further he could do, and then he set off again after a two hour delay. He rang Connie, told her he'd been held up and not to wait up, and arrived home—strange, how he thought of it as home—at ten-thirty.

Connie, however, opened the door and he walked straight into her arms.

'I cooked supper for you.'

'I'm sorry. Thanks for waiting up. There were loads of casualties, I had to help,' he said, burying his face in her hair and inhaling the gorgeous, wicked perfume that seemed to go with her everywhere. 'God, you smell good.'

'You don't. You smell of blood and traffic fumes, but it's good to see you,' she said with a laugh. Tipping back her head, she stretched up and kissed him.

It was like a blow to the solar plexus, and nearly felled him.

'Connie,' he groaned, and went to hold her closer, but she wriggled out of his arms, grabbed his hand and towed him into the kitchen.

'It's only soup—my mother calls it Saturday soup. Fancy some?'

She lifted the lid and he peered in—thick, chunky vegetables and little strips of bacon, and the barest minimum of liquid so that it could be called soup. It smelt fantastic.

'Wow. Give me five to wash and change, and I'll be back.'

He ran upstairs, pulled off his clothes, shot through the shower and went back down in a dressing-gown, just as Connie put the second bowl of steaming broth down on the table.

'Perfect timing,' she said with a smile, and he felt warm to the bottom of his soul.

Strange, how that should hurt.

Connie had waited all day for word, and by eight o'clock she'd been convinced Patrick must arrive at any minute. When he'd phoned to say there'd been an accident on the motorway, her first thought had been that he'd been injured or involved in some way.

Her relief when he'd said he was helping with the injured startled her. So much relief? So much concern?

She'd had a little of the soup because she was starving, but even though he'd told her not to wait up she still didn't go to bed. She hadn't seen him since the morning before, and it seemed light years ago. There was no way she was missing him tonight!

And then he went and showered, and came down all wet and half-dressed, bare legs sticking out the bottom of his dressing-gown, the neck falling open to reveal his chest, and it was too much for her sanity.

She began to talk rubbish, then asked him how he'd got on and shut up. And he told her all about Devon, and how wonderful the other practice was, and how nice Mike and Jane Bryant were, and she went from giddy euphoria to hideous reality in seconds.

Oh, my God, she thought, he really is going to leave, and she had to bite her lip to stop herself from crying out loud.

'So, do you think you'll take the partnership if they offer it to you?' she asked as casually as she could.

He looked at her. She could feel his eyes, but she couldn't look up—not now, with her eyes full of tears.

'I think so,' he said quietly. 'Does it matter?'

'I'll miss you,' she said honestly.

'I'll miss you, too, Connie, but I have to do what's right for us.'

She nodded. 'I know.'

She stood up, clearing the bowls into the dishwasher, and after a few seconds he rose and took the plates out of her hands and turned her into his arms.

'I've missed you this weekend,' he murmured.

A sob caught in her throat, but she stifled it. He tilted her chin and kissed her, and she slid her arms round inside the dressing gown and pressed herself against his chest. Her hands traced the damp column of his spine, flattened over his shoulder blades, feeling the tension in him from the drive. He needed a massage, but there was no way she could dare to risk it.

She eased away, tugging the edges of his dressing gown together again, and stepped back. 'I'm going to bed,' she told him. 'I'll see you in the morning. I'm glad you're back safely.'

And with that she fled to the relative sanctuary of her bedroom.

She heard him come up and check Edward, then go into his room. After a few moments there was silence, then his voice, soft and low, said, 'Goodnight, Connie.'

She didn't reply.

It was one of the longest weeks of Connie's life. She knew he was waiting to hear from Mike Bryant, and she kept busy and out of the way. Edward was set up with Penny now for two days of the week, and Connie spent those two days getting ready for Friday night when her parents came home.

It was wonderful to see them again, and to see her father looking so well. He and Patrick spent a lot of time talking about the practice, and Connie just hoped that if Patrick went it wouldn't be too soon, so her father was thrown back in at the deep end before he was ready.

And then, because she couldn't bear all the hanging about any longer, she packed up her things on Saturday and announced that she was going back to London.

'Edward is already booked with Penny for Monday and Tuesday because I have to see the consultant again and have this scan, and he's there on Wednesday and Friday, anyway, so I'm sure she won't mind having him on Thursday too. That way I can go and sort out what's going to happen with this arm, clear up my flat a little and make some decisions.'

She didn't see Patrick's face, but her mother and father nodded.

'Will you be all right on your own?' her mother asked, fussing as usual.

'Mum, I'm twenty-nine!'

'I know, but—well, with your arm and everything.'

'Mum, I'm fine,' she said firmly. 'I'll be back next weekend. I'll talk to you all then.'

'I'll take you to the station,' Patrick said, but she shook her head.

'I've ordered a taxi. It'll be here at five.'

Patrick opened his mouth to speak, but the phone rang. Mrs Wright answered it, then handed it to Patrick. 'It's for you. Mike Bryant.'

'I'll take it in the surgery, if I may,' he said, and went through.

Connie felt sick. It was a quarter to five, and she was about to go. She hoped to get away before the answer because she just knew they were going to offer him the partnership.

'Oh, please, God,' she mouthed silently.

'Connie, are you all right?' her mother asked.

'I'm fine. I'll just bring my case down.'

She went upstairs and shut her bedroom door. How was she going to bear it? One day at a time, one hour at a time, one minute at a time—

'Connie?'

Patrick opened the door and came in, his face sombre. 'He's offered me the job.'

'I knew he would,' she said, and her voice sounded raw and scratchy. 'Are you going to take it?'

'I think so. I've asked to have till tomorrow night.'

'Why?'

'Because there are other things to consider.'

'Oh,' she replied, wondering if she was one of the other things. 'I have to go—my taxi's here. Will you still be here next weekend?'

'I think so. You are coming back?'

She smiled brightly, knowing it was a lie. 'Of course.'

He drew her into his arms. 'Goodbye, Connie,' he said gruffly, and his lips brushed hers, just lightly.

Then he turned and walked out of her door.

CHAPTER NINE

'PATRICK, could I have a word?'

He looked up from the jigsaw he was doing with Edward. 'Sure. Mrs Wright, would you mind keeping an eye on Edward for a moment?'

'Of course not,' she said, smiling with Connie's smile, and his heart contracted. He missed her already, and it was only Sunday morning.

He followed Dr Wright through into the surgery, and into the consulting room. The older man sat at the desk, in the chair Patrick suddenly realised he'd been beginning to think of as his, and looked around.

'How've you got on here?' Tom asked abruptly.

Patrick wondered what was coming. 'Fine. I like it.'

Tom was doodling now on a freebie pad from a pharmaceutical firm. 'More than Devon?'

That was a loaded question if ever Patrick heard one. 'It's different,' he replied carefully. 'It's a two person practice instead of a one-man band, for a start. It has its advantages, I suppose, but I'm quite happy alone and, on balance, I'd probably rather be here. Why?'

Connie's father looked up from his doodle. 'Because I've decided to retire and sell the practice. I know Connie isn't interested—she's made her feelings about general practice more than clear. I asked her the other day if she'd got any interest in taking over when I retired and she laughed at me. ''When are you going

148

to give up, Dad?'' she said. ''I'm a paediatrician, not a Mr Fix-It.''

'So, I know she doesn't want me to hang on while she trains. That means I have to find a buyer—and I know you're looking for somewhere to buy. I also know, because you told me, that the Devon practice has offered you a partnership, and I know you haven't given them an answer yet. Before you do, I just wanted to give you first refusal on this one.'

Patrick almost pinched himself to see if he was dreaming. It was all his wishes come true—and if he took it, he would still see Connie when she came up to visit her parents, assuming they stayed in the area.

'Is the house included?' he asked, trying to stay calm.

'Oh, yes. The house and surgery all go together. There's a new bungalow just beyond the orchard—we thought we'd buy that. It's very pleasant, easy to run and maintain, no ties and strings. We've had fun together for the past few weeks, and I suddenly realised I didn't want to come back to work. I'm ready to stop, and I've got a sensible pension plan. We can manage, especially with the sale of the practice.'

He stood up and rested his hand on Patrick's shoulder. 'Think about it, son. Talk to Connie.'

'Connie?' he said, puzzled, then shook his head. 'Connie and I aren't…ah…well, we're just not. She's gone back to London.'

'Only for a check-up.'

Patrick shook his head. 'I don't think so. I think she's gone to see what she can do, what contacts she's got to get her back into paediatric medicine. I don't think she'll be coming back.'

'Do you want her to?'

The question was searching and Patrick wasn't sure he wanted to answer it, but his natural honesty wouldn't let him lie. 'Yes—but I know she won't. She's a career doctor. That's what she wants.'

'I wouldn't be so sure,' the older man said thoughtfully. 'I don't think Connie knows what she wants at the moment. She went into surgery after Anthony died, and I'm certain it was just for us—to make up for the fact that we'd lost him.'

'She told me,' Patrick said, remembering the revealing conversation.

He nodded. 'We worried about that because she was happier as a physician, but she's been driven since he died. Maybe this arm injury is just what she needs to set her free. I don't know.'

It was a novel thought, but it didn't change anything. If she went back to paediatric medicine, she would still do it in London. It wouldn't matter if he was up here or down in Devon—except that up here he'd see her from time to time.

Sweet torture, he thought, because it was too far to conduct a romance and expect it to last, and he couldn't go back to London, not to live, not permanently. He'd hated it all the time he'd been there, and couldn't wait to get away, something Marina had found quite unbelievable.

'Do you have any idea how much you want for the practice?' he asked, because that was another consideration, of course. There was no house with the Devon practice, but he would have had to find one. However, with just the two of them it could have been more modest than the Wrights' big four-bedroomed home.

'I've had it valued, but we can always talk about the price. I wouldn't cheat you.'

'I know that. It's just that I don't know if I can afford it.'

'We can discuss it. I can always retain an interest and come in for the odd day. In fact, I might like to do that, if you wouldn't find it an intrusion.'

'Not at all. I wouldn't change anything major, certainly not any of the staff, if you were concerned about that.' He listened to himself as they discussed details, and realised that he was going to accept, regardless of the price.

If it killed him financially to buy it, so be it—it was where he wanted to be.

Even if Connie's image would lurk around every corner…

He took the rest of the afternoon to think about it, although he knew what he wanted to say, because he needed time to consider his relationship with Connie and whether it would be untenable to live there and have her visiting next door, possibly in the future with a husband or boyfriend. Children of her own, maybe.

Oh, God, no.

Not that he wanted to deny her happiness.

He turned into the out-of-hours centre and parked the car, then went in.

'Thank goodness you're here—it's bedlam,' the receptionist told him.

Just what he needed. He shrugged off his jacket, went into the consulting room and hung it on the back of the chair, then pressed the button for the first patient.

He was a man in his sixties, who'd suddenly developed a huge bruise on the front of his biceps.

'Can't understand it,' he said. 'I haven't done anything that I can think of, although I played golf yesterday and felt a little ping in my arm, like twanging a rubber band.'

Patrick nodded, and asked the man to remove his shirt. The two arms could then be compared, and it was immediately obvious that the biceps of the damaged arm was bunched up like a little tennis ball, lower than normal and looking very rounded. Just above the ball-like bump was a very colourful bruise.

'You've ruptured your biceps tendon,' Patrick told him, half his mind on the job and the other half on Connie and whether he should buy the practice. He told the man the bruising would subside, the muscle would continue to function and that he would be fine, although it might look a little odd for a while, and then he sent him away happy.

'Give me a difficult case,' he thought out loud as he reached for the button. 'Something to really take my attention, not just this run-of-the-mill stuff. Something nice and challenging.'

It was not to be. The next patient was a woman with mastitis, suffering from a very sore inflamed breast. It had hot, reddened areas which were very tender, and she was almost in tears with the pain.

'I just don't know what to do,' she wept. 'I can't feed the baby, and she keeps crying and crying!'

'How's the other side?' Patrick asked, gently palpating the affected breast.

'Fine—ouch!'

'Sorry. I think you've got a cracked nipple, which is where the infection has got in, so I want you to do several things. First, I'm going to give you a nice simple antibiotic which should knock this on the head and hopefully won't affect the baby too badly, although she might get the runs a bit and feel a little colicky.

Secondly, I want you to bathe the nipple in warm olive oil with a drop of tea-tree oil in it as a topical anti-bacterial, and thirdly—and I know it sounds like an old wives' tale—but I want you to poultice it with cabbage leaves.'

'What?' she said, looking faintly disbelieving.

He smiled. 'Truly. Just put a few Savoy cabbage leaves in a pan, pour over boiling water, then when they've just wilted lift them out and use them to line your bra. I know it sounds like a second cousin to witchcraft, but I gather it really works.'

She looked sceptical, but promised to try it. 'Frankly, I'll try anything,' she said fervently. 'Can I carry on feeding her?'

He nodded. 'Yes. If you get any pus from the nipple then stop feeding from that side, but I would have thought it would get too painful to feed before that happened. If you use a hot poultice and steam when she's crying to be fed, you'll find the milk will naturally run from the nipple anyway with your let-down reflex, and once it's started flowing the pressure will ease and you should be able to latch the baby on. The idea is to empty the breast completely.'

She nodded. 'I'll try.'

'Fine. And if you have any more problems, go back to your own GP.'

She quickly dressed while he was typing in the details for the prescription, and then left, with a joke about going home via the supermarket for her organic bra-pads and tea-tree oil. 'I might see if they've got eye of newt and leg of toad,' she said with a grin.

'Not in England,' he laughed. 'You need France for frogs' legs.'

Oh, Connie, he thought sadly, I wish I could find you such an easy cure.

She was seeing the consultant the next day. He knew without waiting to hear the results that nothing could be done. It was such a shot in the dark, such a slight chance.

He ached for her, and the steady flow of trivia and general malaise did nothing to distract him.

He arrived back late in the afternoon, and went into the sitting room. The Wrights were there, bracketed by their adoring dogs and smothered in sleeping kittens, with Edward dozing on a chair, and he wondered how they would bear to leave their home.

'I've decided to take the practice on from you, provided we can agree on the price,' he said without preamble.

'I've got a valuation. A man looked at it this summer, and I contacted him the other day and he says the situation hasn't changed. Here are the figures.'

He passed Patrick a piece of paper with the total figure, and a breakdown of the valuation to help him see how it had been arrived at.

'The house would be worth more without the surgery, because that rather spoils it as a straightforward residence, although not for a doctor, of course. It's one of those silly things—and, of course, I can't sell the goodwill. The local health authority have to approve your application to take over the list, but that's a technicality. What do you think?'

He thought he could cope—just—and said so. 'I think it looks very fair. I have to talk to the bank, of course, but I don't see it will be a problem. I've got a fair amount of equity from my house in London, and that's been earning interest. I should be able to make it.'

'Will you mind having Tom peering over your shoulder?' Mrs Wright asked sagely. 'Because he will, of course. He can't leave it alone, whatever he says.'

Patrick chuckled. 'I'm sure I can bear it. I'll have to find him something to do—and rely on you to make sure he gets enough rest.'

'So we're agreed?'

He nodded, and took Tom's extended hand. 'We're agreed. Thank you.'

'No. Thank *you*. You've been wonderful—so helpful and considerate. It's made it all so much easier. I feel as if the practice will be in safe hands—and I really will try very hard not to interfere.'

His wife laughed, stood up and reached for the sherry decanter. 'How about a little drink to seal it?' she said, and Patrick took his glass from her, raised it and sipped. Then he lowered the glass and looked at the Wrights.

'Now all we need is a miracle for Connie,' he said quietly.

'So there's nothing that can be done?'

'I'm sorry, no. The neurologist has studied it closely, and there's no simple quick-fix answer. You'll just have to give it more time and wait—and in the end, I'm afraid, there will still be a fairly substantial neurological deficit.'

Connie nodded, unable to speak for a moment. She hadn't realised how much she'd been banking on a miracle.

'OK. Thanks.'

She stood up, grabbing her bag and heading for the door, but the consultant wasn't finished.

'What will you do now, Connie?'

She hesitated. 'I don't know. Go back to being a physician?'

'Here?'

Suddenly she felt a terrible failure. 'Maybe not. I don't know. Thanks for your help.'

And she all but ran away, hurrying down the corridor, ignoring the old friends and colleagues that hailed her, getting out into the street and walking fast along the pavement. It was too far to walk to her flat, but she did it anyway, letting herself in, making a cup of tea and kicking off her shoes before curling up on one of the chairs in the chilly sitting room and staring at the wall.

She didn't want to cry. Well, she probably did, but she couldn't somehow let go. Her phone rang, and she saw the message light on the answer phone blinking. She let the machine get it, then scooped up the receiver when she realised it was her father.

'Hi. How are things?' she said brightly.

'All right. How are you? What did the consultant say?'

She gulped, suddenly ready to cry after all. 'As we thought,' she said very matter-of-factly. 'There's no quick-fix solution. Dad, I have to go—someone's here. I'll speak to you soon.'

And she hung up the phone, slumped back into the corner of the chair and let go.

'Mrs Bailey! You've lost a bit of weight!'

The young woman chuckled and smiled at him,

clearly very happy. She had a lovely, well baby in her arms, and she showed him off to Patrick proudly.

'He looks fit enough,' he said, settling back in the chair. 'So, what happened? The last time I saw you, you were thirty-two weeks pregnant, huge and very worried. I take it he did have oesophageal atresia?'

She nodded. 'I managed to hang on to thirty-four weeks, but then I was so wretched they took me in and induced me, and the baby had the operation the same day. And it was exactly as Dr Wright's daughter said it would be, and I am just so grateful to her for going through it with me and explaining it so carefully because I knew just what to expect and what they were doing to him.'

'I'll tell her. So, what can I do for you today?' he asked.

She laughed, surprised. 'Nothing. I just came to show him off and to say thank you.' She pulled a box of chocolates out of her bag and handed them to him. 'Perhaps you'd like to share these with Miss Wright. They're from baby Patrick—I hope you don't mind. We borrowed your name.'

Patrick didn't mind at all. Patrick was flattered. He was also wondering if he'd ever get a chance to share the chocolates with Connie, and thought it was probably quite unlikely.

He showed his patient out, put the chocolates in the desk drawer until the end of surgery and carried on.

His next patient also had a baby with a problem, this time a club foot which had been splinted at birth to start the process of correction, and she had come to see him for her six-week check.

He'd never met her before because her antenatal care had been handled by the consultant and the community midwife, but as the consultation proceeded and he talked to her he thought she seemed a little flat.

Because the baby had been born with a slight problem, Patrick wondered if that had pushed her into postnatal depression. He talked to her, and she revealed that she was tired and listless, couldn't find any energy, couldn't be bothered to do anything.

'I just want to take a blood test to make sure you're all right,' he said, and withdrew enough for a whole battery of tests. There might be something clinically wrong with her, and it would be foolish, he thought, to overlook that and just assume that she was depressed because of the baby's foot.

'Julie, I'm going to ask the health visitor to come and see you a bit more often,' he told her, covering his bases. 'I think, with this problem with the baby, you could probably do with a bit more support, and she can answer questions that crop up from day to day.'

And report back to me, he thought, if she's concerned and we turn up nothing. There was nothing in her notes to indicate a predisposition to postnatal depression, but so many cases went undiagnosed, with women suffering needlessly from loneliness and defeat in the early weeks and months of their children's lives.

Sometimes, he knew, it could go on for years before anything was done, and he wanted to make sure that that didn't happen to Julie. At least he knew he'd be here to follow her up, and the knowledge gave him a great sense of satisfaction.

At six, just as he finished, Dr Wright put his head round the door. 'Patrick, are you done?' he asked.

'Yes. There aren't any calls. Why?'

'Connie,' he said flatly, and came in and sat down—

on the patient's chair this time. 'I just rang her a few minutes ago—I've been trying all day without success, and I finally got her. Anyway, it seems the scan wasn't much help. There's nothing they can do.'

He hesitated. 'She sounds—well, rather depressed, to be honest. She was very brief on the phone—said there was someone there, but I think she just didn't want to talk about it.'

'What do you want me to do?' Patrick asked, dreading the answer and yet hoping for it.

'Go and see her. I'm too close, and she may not want to disappoint me or worry me. She's more likely to tell you the truth, I think.'

Jan put her head round the corner of the door. 'I've got someone called Marina on the phone for you, Dr Durrant. Says it's personal.'

He sighed. 'Could you hang on a moment?' he said to Dr Wright. 'This won't take long.'

He picked up the receiver. 'Marina. How was Antigua?'

'Lovely. Bit windy. We had a hurricane, it was frightfully exciting. How's the little monster?'

Monster, indeed. 'Very well. Very happy. Very settled,' he said firmly. 'Don't get any ideas about having him back or visitation rights or custody battles.'

Her tinkling laugh grated on his nerves. 'Oh, Patrick, you're welcome. I still love the little squirt but—you know me—I'm no mother. I just wondered when you were going to collect his stuff. He's got all sorts of things here.'

'I'll do it tomorrow,' he told her. 'Have it all ready by nine o'clock.'

'Will you bring him?'

'No.'

His reply was so unhesitating it shocked even him. 'No, sorry, Marina, he's settled down well with the child-minder. He'll be better here. You can see him by arrangement under supervision in a little while.'

'Fine. Whatever. I'll see you at nine,' she said, and rang off.

Patrick looked up at Connie's father, watching him curiously. 'Will you cover the morning surgery for me tomorrow?' he asked without preamble. 'I'll go down to Connie tonight, talk to her, pick up Edward's stuff tomorrow and come back by lunchtime. I'll see if Penny can have Edward overnight.'

'Don't worry, he's fine here with us. He's a delight. You just go, and give Connie our love. Tell her you're taking over the practice. I didn't get a chance, and it's better done in person.'

Patrick nodded. 'OK. I'll go now.'

'Supper first?'

He shook his head. 'No. I'll get Edward, explain that I have to go to London overnight and then I'll leave.'

So simple. It would have been fine without Edward's tears. 'I don't want you to go! You won't come back!' he sobbed, and Patrick couldn't console him.

'Of course I'll come back,' he assured him. 'I promise.'

'Connie went. I miss Connie. I want her.'

You and me both, Patrick thought grimly. 'I'll go and see Connie and give her your love, and I'm getting all your things from Mummy and bringing them back here. We're going to live here now.'

'With Connie?' he said, a little brighter.

Patrick hesitated. He couldn't lie, but he didn't have

time to go through another bout of tears. 'Maybe,' he procrastinated, knowing it wouldn't be but unable to break Edward's heart. 'Perhaps sometimes.'

If I can drag her away from London for the odd weekend of torment and masochistic self-indulgence.

He kissed Edward goodbye, checked the directions to Connie's flat yet again, then set off. It took just over two hours door to door, and he found a parking slot outside by a miracle. He went into the foyer of the tall, forbidding building, pressed the intercom button and waited.

Connie couldn't believe it. Just when she'd crawled into the bath, the doorbell rang. She crawled out, wrapped her towel round her against the chill and went to the door, pressing the button. 'Yes?'

'Connie, it's Patrick.'

The breath whooshed out of her lungs, and she sagged against the wall.

'Connie?'

'Come up,' she said unsteadily, pressing the button, and she heard the door downstairs click, then his firm, heavy tread on the stairs. She opened the flat door and let him in.

'I'm sorry, I got you out of the bath,' he began, but she didn't care about it any more. She didn't care about anything except being in his arms, and she threw herself at him with a strangled cry.

'Patrick!' she sobbed, and all the pent-up tears and anguish and expectation and pressure which had been with her since Anthony's death came out in a huge rush of tears.

'Oh, Connie,' he said gruffly, and wrapped her tight

against his chest, rocking her from side to side and saying her name over and over again.

Finally the first rush of tears abated, and she pulled herself together and eased away from him. His soft suede leather jacket was blotched with her tears, and she dabbed ineffectually at the marks.

He took her hand—her right hand—and lifted it to his lips. 'I'm sorry. I gather the news wasn't good.'

She shook her head. 'I just feel lost. I knew where I was going before. Now I feel like I've been cast adrift and I just don't know where I'll end up.'

She sniffed, scrubbed her nose on her hand and looked for a tissue. Patrick put one in her hand and she blew her nose loudly and tried for a smile. 'Sorry. It was all a bit awful, and I've missed you…'

The smile wobbled, and his face seemed to crumple as he reached for her. 'Oh, love, I've missed you, too.'

His mouth found hers, and Connie felt as if she'd come home.

There was no hesitation this time, not for either of them. She slipped her arms round his waist under his jacket and snuggled close, and she felt a groan rumble through his chest.

'Connie, I want you,' he whispered hoarsely. 'Let me make love to you.'

'Oh, Patrick,' she said, and her eyes overflowed again. 'I've missed you so much. I came back here and I needed you so badly.'

'Oh, Connie…' She thought he was going to crush her, but then his arms slackened just long enough to shift his grip and swing her up against his chest like a child. 'Where's the bedroom?' he asked tautly.

'Through there.' She waved at the doorway, and he shouldered the door out of the way and dropped her into the middle of the hastily made bed. It was freezing, the sheets chilly against her back, and he pulled the covers back, lifted her and dispensed with the towel, dropping her inside the bed before tearing off his clothes and sliding in beside her.

There were no words, no need for words. It was just so right to be there with him, holding him, letting him touch her like this. He was almost rough with her, his trembling hands exploring her with eager haste, and yet he was still careful, never rough to the point of hurting her.

She felt the pressure building, felt the blood pounding in her veins as he moved over her, then he was part of her and her soul cried out to his.

The streetlights slanted across the ceiling, casting strange shadows on the wall. Connie watched them for a moment, her eyes adjusting to the darkness, and beside her she felt Patrick stir.

'Connie?' he murmured.

'Mmm?'

His mouth found hers in the half-dark, sipping and teasing. 'Are you OK?' he asked gently. 'That got a little wild.'

'I'm fine—never better. You?'

He laughed softly. 'Oh, definitely never better. I know it sounds like a cliché, but it's true, Connie, I swear.' His hand cupped her cheek, and he kissed her again, just very lightly. 'I love you,' he said, and a huge knot in her chest balled up even tighter.

'I love you, too. I think I have for ages, but we're just going such different ways. You're going to Devon, and I haven't a clue what the hell I'm doing—' She broke off, choked by tears again, and she felt him shift, propping himself up on the pillows and drawing her into his arms.

'Actually, I'm not going to Devon,' he told her in a careful voice.

She didn't understand. He'd been so keen...

'Why?' she asked, puzzled. 'I thought you liked it.'

'I did—but your father's decided to go early. He's offered me the practice, and I've said yes.'

'Oh.' Shock transfixed her for a moment, and she struggled to sit up. 'Um—the house as well?'

'Yes. They're buying that new bungalow just at the end of the garden beyond the orchard.'

So she was losing her home, too!

'That's nice,' she said blandly, flailing for something to say. Suddenly she felt terribly alone, terribly lost. What had this all meant?

If anything?

'Is that all?' he asked. 'Just nice?'

She sniffed. 'It's my home. I feel a bit strange about losing it.'

He was quiet for a long time, then he said, very softly, 'What if you didn't have to lose it? What if you were to live there?'

'Me? But you're buying it for you.'

'Maybe for us,' he said, and she could hear a touch of uncertainty in his voice. 'You could do paediatrics in Ipswich or Colchester, maybe, and I wouldn't expect you to give up your career.'

She laughed. 'What career? Patrick, I don't have a career.'

'Not at the moment, maybe, but you could have, Connie, given time. And if you wanted that, I would never stand in your way. I don't want a mother for Edward. For better or worse, he's got a mother. What

I want is someone who cares for him and me, to share our lives. I don't want a servant—I don't want you to think that. It's nothing to do with him. And I know you don't want to be a GP, Connie, but how about being a GP's wife?'

'Wife?' she said, a little dazed.

'Yes, wife,' he confirmed. 'I'm asking you to marry me, Connie—and I hope to God you're going to say yes.'

CHAPTER TEN

CONNIE didn't know whether to laugh or cry, so she solved the problem by doing both.

'Oh, yes, yes, yes!' she said, happiness bubbling up inside her and swamping all the worry and uncertainty.

Patrick hesitated for a second, staring at her in disbelief, and then engulfed her in the biggest hug she'd ever had.

'Oh, Connie, thank God!' he whispered raggedly. 'Thank God.'

She hugged him back, sniffing and smiling and blinking all at once. She wasn't going to lose him! Strange, how much more important that seemed than not being able to go back to surgery. And she'd have Edward, too, with his delicious giggle she was hearing more and more these days.

'And, of course, I'll look after Edward,' she added, pushing him away so she could look him in the eye. Too dark. She sat up and snapped on the bedside light, rummaged under the pillow for her nightdress and tugged it on, then wriggled up beside him again.

'It's amazing how things look different in different lights,' she told him. 'For instance, only a couple of hours ago I was so miserable, because I was here all alone, you were going to Devon and I was never going to see you again. Now I'm going to marry you. You can have no idea how suddenly incredibly unimportant my arm seems. I don't care if it never gets any better. I can learn to cope with what sensation and control

166

I've got, and as long as I'm with you and Edward what more could I possibly want?'

'But you're a career doctor,' he said, sounding confused.

'Am I?' she said wryly, thinking about it. 'I don't think so. Anyway, a career's a very fragile thing, as I've proved. Other things are much more important.'

'So you don't want to go back to work?'

She shrugged. 'Maybe, one day. I'm quite happy to work, especially if we need the money, but I don't feel I have to for the sake of my soul or anything crazy like that. In fact,' she said with a sly smile, trailing her fingers over his chest, 'I'd be quite happy to work on giving Edward a little brother or sister to play with. What do you think?'

Patrick grinned, clearly relieved. 'What—now?'

She met his eyes, and the laughter in them died, replaced by a simmering heat which had never been far away when he looked at her. 'Why not?' she said softly. 'Got a better idea?'

He gave a wry chuckle. 'Not really. Come here, let me warm you up, you're freezing. You won't conceive if you're cold.' He snuggled her down in his arms, kissed her lingeringly and brushed the hair back from her face, while she stared up at him and thought she'd never seen anyone more wonderful in her life.

'I love you,' he murmured, all trace of humour fading. 'I want you to know that.'

'I do know,' she said. 'I'd have to be blind not to see it in your eyes at the moment. They're transparent at the best of times. Just now you couldn't keep a secret from me in the dark.'

He gave a soft laugh and hugged her close. 'Oh,

Connie, I don't want to have any secrets from you. I just want to be with you and hold you.'

'Good. Hold away, because I feel just the same. I love you, Patrick.'

His lips found hers, and there was no more conversation for a while. They had better things to do than talk.

'Why don't you come back with me in the morning?' he asked later, when they'd started talking again.

She shook her head. They were sitting cross-legged on the sofa, face to face, a newly delivered Chinese take-away on the cushion between them, feeding each other strips of chicken and noodles. It was messy, but fun. Connie was allowed a fork instead of chopsticks as she was already disadvantaged, and because Patrick didn't want to starve to death he allowed her to cheat.

'Why not?' he asked round a king prawn.

'Because I have things to do. I have to pack up my flat, and go and resign and talk to my boss, and just sort out my life here. Say goodbye to it.'

He nodded. He did understand, but he would miss her. 'How long will you need?' he asked.

'A few days. You could pick me up at the weekend, if you're offering?'

'Done. I want that bit of pepper.'

'Please.'

'Please.'

She dropped it down his front, then giggled as he rolled his eyes. He could remember a time when she would have stormed off in a rage or burst into tears, and he picked the pepper up and put it in his mouth, smiling as he chewed it. 'Can you manage to pack up on your own?'

She tipped her head on one side thoughtfully. 'Oh, I expect so. I might have to get the odd male colleague to help me.'

He studied her. Was she joking? He'd never asked, but there might have been someone in her life, someone who cared, someone who might feel pushed out by his presence.

'No,' she said firmly, reading his mind. 'There's no one. I'm teasing. There hasn't been anyone for years and years.'

He tried not to sigh too obviously with relief, but apparently he failed. 'Such a fragile ego,' she teased.

'You didn't have to live with Marina,' he said by way of explanation.

Her face sobered. 'Was it awful?' she asked quietly.

'Sometimes,' he said honestly, remembering the rows. 'Either we were fighting about something trivial or she was out shopping. Fortunately she had her own income—an allowance from her father, who's disgustingly wealthy—so I wasn't having to subsidise her retail therapy sessions. It also meant I got the house which I already owned, which is how come I'm able to buy the practice. And, of course, without having to pay maintenance for Edward I should be better off—'

'I don't need a breakdown of your bank balance,' Connie teased, and he relaxed.

'Sorry. I was just filling you in.'

'Don't worry. If you need me to work, I'll work.'

He smiled and shook his head. 'I don't. We'll manage.'

'Even if I'm pregnant?'

She looked beautiful and impish and sassy, and he wanted her all over again. 'Even if you're pregnant,' he said gruffly, and wondered how much more of the food he was going to have to eat before he could decently carry her back to bed.

'Hi, Andy.'

Andy Crossley, Connie's boss, looked up from his notes and stared, then took off his glasses and threw them down, before coming round the desk to hug her.

'Connie, my dear girl, how are you? Sara told me the news. I'm so sorry.'

She smiled. Funny, she didn't care any more. 'Thanks, Andy, but you needn't be. In fact, you can congratulate me. I'm getting married to my father's locum, who's taking over his practice, so I'm going to end up living with him in my childhood home, bringing up his little boy and having lots more little Durrants.'

Andy peered down at her, blinking to focus at such close range. 'And is that what you really want?' he asked carefully. 'Will it be enough, Connie?'

She thought of the night she'd just spent with Patrick, and smiled again, more broadly this time. 'Oh, yes, it'll be enough,' she assured Andy. 'Truly. Anyway, I'm here officially to hand in my notice and resign, although you must have known I was about to.'

He nodded. 'Yes. I spoke to Sara yesterday. She told me to expect it. I can't deny I'm sorry, you had the makings of a hell of a surgeon, but you look happier today than you've looked for ages. Whoever this guy is, I hope he's worthy of you.'

Her chuckle drove the doubt from his eyes. 'He's wonderful. Stop worrying about me. Patrick and my father can do that now—you're off the hook, Andy.'

'Well, I wish you luck. When's the wedding?'

She shrugged. 'I don't know. He only asked me last night. We haven't had time to think about it.'

'Give me an invitation. I'd like to see you settled in your new career. You deserve a break.'

'Andy, you're a love. Thanks for everything,' she said, hugging him, and then left him to it because his first patient was outside and he needed to start his clinic.

She found other members of staff about the place, some in the clinic, some on the ward, and made her farewells with a light heart. There were some sad moments, old friends she'd missed in the past few weeks whom she might never see again, others who themselves were moving on.

In busy hospitals nothing stood still for long, and the waters would soon close over her head, leaving not a ripple.

She went back to her flat, rang the agent and was told there was someone desperate who would gladly take over her tenancy. Could she be out by tomorrow? Immediate refund of all overpaid rent including the whole of October, as an incentive, because the rent was going up for the new tenant.

Considering it was already the last week in October, she thought that was absurdly generous.

'I'll do it,' she said, 'but pay the rent to the Great Ormond Street Hospital for me, could you? For their neonatal research unit.'

The agent clearly thought she was mad, and so she might be, but it was money she hadn't expected to have back and it was a sort of pay-off, an offering to the gods for saving her life.

Off with the old and on with the new, she thought, putting the phone down. Then she looked around, grabbed the phone again and rang Patrick on his mobile.

'Where are you?' she asked.

'Near Tower Bridge, on my way home. She wasn't ready, of course, and there's so much stuff it's ridiculous. We'll have to come down and sort it all out and give most of it to charity. I expect Great Ormond Street could use most of the toys and things.'

She laughed.

'What's funny?' he asked, sounding puzzled.

'Nothing. Remind me to tell you about my rent refund. So, if you're not taking the stuff now, does that mean you've got an empty car?'

'More or less,' he said cautiously. 'Why?'

'Because I'm coming home,' she told him. 'I've let my flat, and they want to move in tomorrow. Can you pick me and my junk up?'

She could hear the smile right down the phone. 'I'll be with you in half an hour,' he vowed, and she cradled the phone, smiled sappily for a second, and then started packing like there was no tomorrow.

'I gather you're getting married at the end of the year,' Mrs Pike the younger said.

He nodded. 'Yes, to Dr Wright's daughter Connie.'

Ann Pike smiled. 'Nice girl. I'm glad she's come home. We were all ever so upset when her brother died, and she hasn't been the same since. I saw her in the shop yesterday, and she looked happier than I've seen her for such a long time. You've done her good.'

Patrick felt his colour rise a little. 'Thank you. She's done me and my son good, too. She's a darling. I shall take good care of her.'

Ann laughed. 'Mind you do. We'll all be watching you.'

Patrick glanced up the quiet hall towards the elder Mrs Pike's room. 'All quiet on the western front,' he said softly. 'Headphones working?'

There was a throaty chuckle from the woman. 'Marvellous. I love you for that. Best thing that's happened to us in ages. There's something else as well. Come and see her.'

They went in, and Mrs Pike took off her headphones and put them down, then fiddled with her ear.

'Hello, Mrs Pike,' Patrick yelled, and the old woman screwed up her face.

'Don't shout,' she all but whispered. 'I've got this internal new hearing aid you insisted I should get—you wouldn't believe how much noise this girl makes, crashing about with the vacuum cleaner in here. I have to turn it down so I don't go deaf!'

He stifled a smile. 'How's the hip?' he asked.

'Wonderful. You lied, young man. You told me I'd be crippled for life, and I'm no such thing! Better than I've been for years! Look!'

And she stood up and started marching round the room, showing off her new hip.

He said nothing. There was no point in arguing—he couldn't possibly win. She just moved the goalposts.

'That's marvellous,' he told her, trying to remember not to shout, and examined her to make sure she was really as well as she said.

'I gather you're marrying young Connie,' she said, fixing him with a gimlet eye as he folded his stethoscope. 'Mind you take care of her. We all love Connie, don't we, Ann?'

'Yes, Mum,' Ann said patiently. 'I just told him so.'

'She did, and I promised to look after her,' he assured her.

'Well, mind you do. We'll be watching.'

You and everybody else in Great Ashley, he thought with a chuckle as he left them. You and everybody else.

The health authority rubber-stamped Patrick as the new holder of the practice, the bank was happy to play ball, and a couple of weeks before Christmas Patrick officially took over and the Wrights moved into their new home.

Connie helped them, in between planning for their wedding which was to take place between Christmas and New Year.

'We'll never manage everything at once, it'll be such a rush!' Mrs Wright protested. 'You always were so impulsive. Why couldn't you wait for a nice summer wedding, so we don't all have to wear coats and gloves and woolly hats?'

Connie laughed and unwrapped another glass bowl. 'Woolly hats are cute,' she told her mother. 'And, anyway, we don't want to wait. It's better for all of us to do it sooner. Now, are you sure we can manage the reception? I don't want you taking on too much.'

'Well, it won't be too much, will it, with Christmas and New Year each side of it so most of our relations can't come?'

'Mum, we just want a quiet wedding,' Connie said for the thousandth time. 'Just a few family and friends to give us a bit of a send-off. Nothing wild and flashy.'

'But Aunty Rose—'

'Is an interfering busybody, and I'm quite happy to

get married without her. We'll send her a big piece of cake.'

Her mother tutted. 'Connie, that's not nice. You know she can't eat it without getting indigestion!'

Connie smiled sweetly. 'Oh, yes. I'd forgotten.'

'Connie!'

She relented. 'Mum, you've only just moved. Dad hasn't been well at all, Patrick's up to his ears with taking over the practice—we don't need a lot of fuss. None of us need it. I just want to get married, that's all. I'd be quite happy with just the five of us there.'

She unwrapped the last bowl, checked the bottom of the box and took it off the table. 'Right, that's everything unpacked now. How about the bed? If we make it up, you can turn in as early as you like. I expect you're exhausted.'

Connie's mother looked round her new kitchen and sighed quietly. 'It seems so strange. We've been in the other house so long now.'

She hugged her. 'Mum, you'll soon get used to it. Your knees were finding the stairs a bit much, and Dad's better off here by miles. And, anyway, it's not like you've sold it to strangers! You can come up there any time you like, you know that. You can come and cook with Edward and practise being a grandma.'

Her mother snorted. 'I don't suppose there's much point. You'll both be too busy to have children for ages.'

Connie stifled a smile. 'We've got Edward already, don't forget. He needs a grandma.'

Her face softened. 'So he does. He's a darling. So's Patrick. I'm really happy for you, Connie. I just hope it all works out.'

'I'm sure it will,' Connie said with deep confidence. 'Now, let's do this bed so you can fall in it!'

They decided to celebrate Christmas at the Wrights' new home. It was a funny mixture of old and new because all the furniture was from the old house, yet arranged in a different way, of course. The Christmas tree was in the corner by the French doors, and there was a lovely view of the garden.

At least, it would be a lovely view one day. Now it was all turf and bare earth borders, except for the gnarled old apple tree at the end which the builder had left.

Not that anyone minded that Christmas morning. They were all too busy, looking under the tree for presents. At least, Edward was, and Connie was down there helping him.

'Here, there's one for you,' she said, handing a little package to Patrick.

He opened it and pulled out a lovely soft leather wallet, just like his old one but not falling to pieces.

'Oh, Connie, thank you,' he said with a smile.

'It's got the same pockets and things.'

'I noticed. That's the worst thing about changing them. That's why I haven't done it.'

'That's why I sneaked yours down to the local saddler and got him to make you a replacement,' she grinned.

He laughed and hugged her. 'Crafty minx. I can see I'll have to watch you.'

'Mmm. Very likely. It's not your main present. You'll have to wait for that.'

'I don't want to wait,' he complained.

She smiled and looked over her shoulder. The others were all busy unwrapping Edward's electric car. 'Well, you'll have to. It's one of these things that can't be hurried. You'll have to wait—let's see—not quite seven months now.'

He stared at her for an age, and then light dawned in his eyes. 'Connie?' he said softly, and she could see the wonder blossoming on his face.

'Yes,' she said with a contented smile. 'So I just hope we can manage without my income, because I'm going to be a full-time mother from now on.'

His eyes misted, and he blinked and tipped his head back and gave a little cough of laughter. 'You certainly know how to blindside a man,' he said with a smile when he'd recovered his composure a bit. 'Do they know?'

He glanced across at her parents, and she shook her head.

'No. I wanted to tell you first,' she said, and kissed him. 'Happy Christmas, darling.'

'I shall enjoy sorting the garden out,' her father said, standing at the window after lunch. 'A challenge.'

'You take it easy,' Connie threatened him. 'You've been warned—just don't overdo it.'

He turned and folded her gently against his still-tender chest. 'I won't—at least not for a while. Oh, Connie, I can't believe everything's working out so well. You marrying Patrick next week, him taking over the practice, knowing you're going to still be in the house—we've got so much to be thankful for.'

'And your health,' she said, tipping back her head and looking up at him. 'Don't forget your health.'

He smiled gently. 'I won't. Right, come on, everyone, it's time to play a game. What shall we start with?'

'How about Happy Families?' Connie said with a smile.

The day of their wedding dawned wet and cold and dismal. Connie opened the curtains of her parents' spare bedroom and looked out, then groaned.

Her mother tapped on the door and came in with a cup of tea. 'Just look at it! I told you you should have had a summer wedding!' she said, lowering herself to the edge of the bed. 'I've brought you tea.'

Connie took it, looked at it and put it down on the bedside table. 'Well, we could have done,' she said with a smile, 'but I thought you'd rather be a mother-in-law before you were a grandmother.'

Her mother's eyes widened. 'Connie?' she said incredulously. 'You're not!'

'I am,' she said, very happily. 'We're delighted.'

'Does Patrick know?'

'Of course. He's thrilled. He can hardly wait. And I want to see Dad's face, because it's his fault, you know. He sent Patrick down to talk to me when I'd seen the consultant, and that's when it happened, so he needn't go all disapproving because he won't get away with it.'

Her mother laughed. 'Connie, darling, I don't think he's about to go all disapproving, as you put it! You're nearly thirty, after all. We were beginning to despair of ever being grandparents.'

She looked at the cup of tea. 'Um—do you want that?'

Connie laughed and shook her head. 'Not really.'

I'm all right, but I do get a little queasy sometimes. Perhaps some really cold spring water?'

Her mother stood up and took the cup away. 'Done. Are you going to get up? You've got a lot to do before the wedding.'

Connie yawned and stretched. 'I suppose so. I hope my dress still fits. I'm getting a bit busty.'

'Well, at least being a winter dress it's not low cut, so you won't fall out of the top right under the vicar's nose!'

She slipped out of bed, drank some mineral water, showered and washed and dried her hair, then put on her make-up. It felt strange to wear it, but she'd been practising putting it on with her right hand and her left, and between the two she'd just about got it sorted out. That wasn't the only thing she'd been practising, but she'd have to wait and see if she'd done enough.

Her mother appeared in her room, dressed in a royal blue fine wool suit dress. She looked lovely, and Connie told her so.

'Thank you, darling. Right, let's see if we can still squeeze you in. I see what you mean,' she added, peering at Connie's somewhat lusher curves under the lace of her bra. She took the silk taffeta dress off the hanger, shook it out and held it open for Connie to step into it.

Connie wriggled her arms down the sleeves, lifted the shoulders up over her own and held her breath as her mother slid the zip up.

'You're in,' her mother said, and Connie sighed with relief.

'Thank goodness for that. I've only got half an hour, so there isn't time to fiddle. Right, how about my veil?

Can you anchor it for me? I still don't trust these hands to do it properly.'

Her mother positioned the simple little headdress, pinned it to Connie's hair and then arranged her veil.

'Give me a twirl,' she said, and Connie stood up, slipped on her shoes and turned slowly round.

'Oh, darling, you look wonderful!' her mother said, going misty-eyed. 'Tom, come and see.'

Her father came in, dressed in his best dark suit and looking so like Anthony her eyes filled.

'Oh, Connie,' he said, and then hovered.

'What?'

'I was going to hug you, but I daren't rumple everything.'

Connie gave a strangled laugh and threw herself into her father's arms. 'I can be unrumpled,' she told him.

'Tom, congratulate her—you're going to be a grandfather,' his wife told him, picking fluff off his shoulder.

He released his daughter, look at her for confirmation and then hugged her again. 'I wondered,' he said, putting her down at last. 'You have that bovine look women get.' He smiled. 'Can I take the credit for pushing you together?'

'Don't you mean the blame?' Connie teased. 'You realise everybody in the village is going to be watching us and counting months. We'd managed to be circumspect until you sent Patrick down to me.'

'Let them count,' her father said proudly. 'You love each other. That's what matters. Anyway, Anthony was premature, so to speak.'

Connie chuckled, then her smile faded. 'I wish he could be here.'

'Don't we all?' her mother said softly. 'He'd be very proud of you, Connie—very proud indeed. And he'd approve of Patrick.'

Connie nodded, not quite steady enough to speak.

Tom Wright cleared his throat. 'Well, I suppose it's time to get this show on the road.'

It had seemed silly to book a car to take her such a short distance to the church, but there was someone in the village who did wedding cars, and he'd offered it for nothing. It turned out he was the father of the little girl whose life Connie had saved when she had epiglottitis and was choking, and as they arrived at the church, he pointed out his wife and daughter to her, standing in the churchyard.

'There they are. Looks a bit different now, doesn't she?'

'She certainly does,' Connie said, suddenly so glad she'd had the nerve to do the simple and yet terrifying operation.

She climbed carefully out of the car, holding her skirts high, and smiled at the young woman and the wide-eyed toddler.

'I hope you don't mind us coming, but I just wanted to thank you so much, Dr Wright,' the woman said. 'You look absolutely beautiful. Doesn't she look lovely, Beth?'

Beth nodded, and Connie laughed and bent over. '*You* look a bit better than you did,' she said, studying the tiny mark on the child's throat, then she straightened up.

There were other people there she recognised—old Mrs Pike, with her new hip and her hearing aid, and the old postmistress Mrs Grimwade, from whom they had got the kittens, and—oh, so many others, standing there in the damp winter morning to see her.

'Thank you for turning out to see us married,' she said to them all, and then looked up at her father.

'Are you ready?' he asked.

She nodded, and he straightened her veil, tweaked her nose and held out his arm. 'Come on, then, let's go and give you away.'

The organist struck up as they entered the church, and Connie thought she was going to cry when she saw Edward waiting for her with her mother. He was dressed in a little suit, holding a satin cushion in his hands, and gave her a wobbly smile.

'Hi, darling,' she said, and bent down and kissed him. 'Are you all ready to help with the rings?'

He nodded. 'You look really pretty, Connie,' he told her, and she nearly cried again.

'Thanks, pumpkin. You don't look so bad yourself. Daddy there, waiting for me?'

He nodded. 'He said I'm not to let you run away.'

She laughed out loud, and everyone turned round and looked at her, grinning. 'I'm not going anywhere except to him,' she assured her little page.

Her mother slipped down the aisle into her seat, the congregation waited expectantly and Connie took a steadying breath. 'Right. Let's go for it.'

Patrick thought he was going to die of suspense. He heard the music strike up, heard Connie's laugh and the ripple of amusement that ran through the congregation and then he couldn't stand it any longer.

He turned, looking down the length of the aisle to the woman he loved more than his wildest imaginings, and swallowed a huge lump in his throat.

She looked stunning. Slender, graceful, her eyes shining behind the simple veil, the delicate blooms of her posy setting off the colour of her hair and the honey-gold of her eyes.

Where she'd found freesias in December he didn't know, nor did he care. He just wanted her there by his side, the wedding over, their lives together beginning.

She returned his smile, and he realised he was grinning like an idiot. So what? He adored her.

She reached his side, and he winked and squeezed her hand. She threaded her fingers through his and hung on, and he could feel tension in her.

However, her vows were strong and firm, as were his, and he couldn't understand her nerves. His were over now, banished by her lovely smile and the look in her eyes.

They had to move apart so that Edward could stand in front of them with his little cushion. Patrick's best man fished the rings out of his pocket and put them on the cushion, and Edward stuck his tongue in the corner of his mouth and concentrated very hard while the vicar took the rings from the cushion and put them on the Bible in his hands.

He blessed them, then Patrick repeated his vow and put the ring on Connie's finger.

Her hands were shaking now, and then suddenly he realised why when she lifted her right hand. She picked up his ring between her slow, unresponsive thumb and nerveless index finger, very carefully and deliberately. Grabbing his ring finger with her left hand to steady herself, she painstakingly pushed the ring onto his finger and slid it home.

Then her shoulders dropped, her head came up and she laughed softly with relief.

'I am so proud of you,' Patrick said, completely ignoring the vicar. He lifted her veil, put it carefully back over her head and reached for her. 'I love you, Connie,' he whispered. Then his lips found hers, his arms crushed her against him and he lifted her clean off the ground.

In the background, the vicar carried on. 'Those whom God hath joined together, let no man put asunder.' Then he looked down at their heads, so close together as Patrick released her, and said, 'You may kiss the bride—again!'

And everybody laughed and cheered. Everybody, that is, except Patrick and Connie. Patrick had picked Edward up in one arm, put the other round Connie and hugged her, kissing her briefly and respectably this time.

They were married. A new start, both for Connie and for him and Edward, and for the new baby.

A new start for the practice, and for Connie's parents, too.

Soon it would be the new year, and a new era.

What a wonderful start, he thought and, turning to Connie, he met her eyes and smiled.

'I love you, Dr Durrant,' he told her.

'I love you, too, Dr Durrant,' she said, grinning.

'That's silly,' Edward said. 'You'll have to call her Connie or everyone will get in a muddle.'

'I think I'll just be Mrs Durrant,' she said contentedly.

Patrick's smile widened even further. 'Sounds good to me,' he said. 'Sounds absolutely perfect.'

MILLS & BOON®

Makes any time special

Enjoy a romantic novel from
Mills & Boon®

Presents...™ *Enchanted™* TEMPTATION.

Historical Romance™ ✛MEDICAL ROMANCE™

MILLS & BOON

MEDICAL
ROMANCE

A FAMILIAR FEELING by Margaret Barker

Dr Caroline Bennett found working at the Chateau Clinique with Pierre, the boy she'd adored as a child, wasn't easy. It didn't help that his ex-wife was still around.

HEART IN HIDING by Jean Evans

Dr Holly Hunter needed respite, and the remote Scottish village was ideal. Until Callum McLoud turned up accusing her of treating his patients!

HIS MADE-TO-ORDER BRIDE by Jessica Matthews
Bachelor Doctors

Dr J.D. Berkely had a good job in ER, a delightful son Daniel, and a truly good friend in nurse Katie Alexander, so why would he need a wife?

A TIMELY AFFAIR by Helen Shelton

Dr Merrin Ryan sees that widowed Professor Neil McAlister needs nurturing and she falls in love! But Neil is aware that he could damage her career…

Available from 5th November 1999

Available at most branches of WH Smith, Tesco, Martins, Borders, Easons, Volume One/James Thin and most good paperback bookshops

COMING NEXT MONTH

MILLS & BOON®

Presents...

MARRIAGE ULTIMATUM *by Lindsay Armstrong*

Neve couldn't work out why Rob Stowe was suddenly insisting upon marrying her, or whether she should even say 'yes' when the mother of his child was still so much in evidence!

MISTRESS BY ARRANGEMENT *by Helen Bianchin*

Nikos Alessandros needed a social hostess and Michelle needed a male companion to deter an unwanted suitor. A convenient affair—if they can keep their passions in check!

BARTALDI'S BRIDE *by Sara Craven*

Guido Bartaldi had obviously decided upon his reluctant ward as his wife. When Clare accepted a position with him she began to suspect that Guido had an entirely different set of intentions!

BOUGHT: ONE HUSBAND *by Diana Hamilton*

In her innocence Alissa offered to pay Jethro Cole to marry her, to comply with the conditions of her uncle's will. In fact Jethro was a millionaire intent on making Alissa his own.

Available from 5th November 1999

*Available at most branches of WH Smith, Tesco, Martins,
Borders, Easons, Volume One/James Thin
and most good paperback bookshops*

COMING NEXT MONTH

MILLS & BOON®

Presents...™

THE SOCIETY GROOM *by Mary Lyons*
(Society Weddings)

Once, they'd had a passionate affair. When they met again at a society wedding Olivia thought she'd lost all interest in Dominic FitzCharles—until he made a surprise announcement...

SLADE BARON'S BRIDE *by Sandra Marton*
(The Barons)

When Lara Stevens met Slade Baron an overnight flight delay led to a tempting invitation. Who would Lara hurt if she accepted? He wanted her and she wanted...a baby.

GIBSON'S GIRL *by Anne McAllister*

Gibson was fascinated by the shy and beautiful Chloe. Should he seduce her? Gib was tempted. Should she resist him? Chloe had to. Eventually it became a question of who was seducing whom!

MARRIAGE ON TRIAL *by Lee Wilkinson*

Elizabeth had insisted on an annulment - and disappeared from Quinn's life. Now he'd tracked her down and claimed she was still his wife. Did he really love her, or did he want revenge?

Available from 5th November 1999

Available at most branches of WH Smith, Tesco, Martins, Borders, Easons, Volume One/James Thin and most good paperback bookshops

Spoil yourself next month
with these four novels from

TEMPTATION®

IN THE DARK by Pamela Burford

Wrong Bed

Cat Seabright had a 'baby-making' date with her best friend's cousin. But in the middle of a blackout in a dark hotel room, she realized she was in bed with a passionate stranger. A stranger who, in the light of day, wanted much, much more than a one night stand!

HER DESPERADO by Alyssa Dean

Lacy Johnson would do a lot of things to keep her ranch out of the bank's clutches. But marrying her gorgeous neighbour Morgan Brillings wasn't one of them. She was determined to turn down his proposal of a marriage of convenience—just as soon as she got out of his bed…

SINGLE, SEXY…AND SOLD! by Vicki Lewis Thompson

Bachelor Auction

Hunky fireman Jonah Hayes performed heroic acts every day. But little did he guess that rescuing a puppy would land him on the auction block! Or that he'd be sold to sexy Natalie Leblanc, the puppy's owner, who was intent on showing him just how grateful she was!

BREATHLESS by Kimberly Raye

Blaze

Ten years ago, Tack Brandon had left his first love Annie Divine. Now he was back and Annie was ready to get even. She might offer Tack her bed again…but never her heart. She planned to love him within an inch of his life and then walk away…

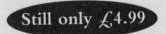
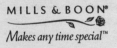

2 FREE
books and a surprise gift!

We would like to take this opportunity to thank you for reading this Mills & Boon® book by offering you the chance to take TWO more specially selected titles from the Medical Romance™ series absolutely FREE! We're also making this offer to introduce you to the benefits of the Reader Service™—

- ★ FREE home delivery
- ★ FREE gifts and competitions
- ★ FREE monthly Newsletter
- ★ Exclusive Reader Service discounts
- ★ Books available before they're in the shops

Accepting these FREE books and gift places you under no obligation to buy, you may cancel at any time, even after receiving your free shipment. Simply complete your details below and return the entire page to the address below. *You don't even need a stamp!*

YES! Please send me 2 free Medical Romance books and a surprise gift. I understand that unless you hear from me, I will receive 4 superb new titles every month for just £2.40 each, postage and packing free. I am under no obligation to purchase any books and may cancel my subscription at any time. The free books and gift will be mine to keep in any case.

M9EA

Ms/Mrs/Miss/Mr ....Initials..................................
                                                        BLOCK CAPITALS PLEASE
Surname ....
Address ....
....
....Postcode...................................

Send this whole page to:
UK: FREEPOST CN81, Croydon, CR9 3WZ
EIRE: PO Box 4546, Kilcock, County Kildare (stamp required)